"Shall we dance?"

He ran his thumb along her palm, drawing her in.

For a moment she forgot how to breathe. But wasn't this what she wanted? Her last chance to dance with him? "I thought you'd never ask."

As he led her to the dance floor, she noticed the stares of his family members.

"Ignore them," he whispered, pulling her into his arms. "Pretend it's just you and me out here. Just like old times."

She could do that. She'd been pretending for such a long time that she was practically an expert.

You wanted this, remember?

She did. She'd wanted to dance with him since the second he walked into the ballroom. She belonged in his arms. But now that it was happening, she wondered... Had dancing with him always felt so... intimate?

There was no other word for it. His face was only a breath away. His heart beat against her chest. And the skillful way he moved made her weak in the knees.

If this was what it felt like to dance with Zander Wilde, what would it feel like to go to bed with him?

* * *

WILDE HEARTS:
Letting their hearts loose, one Wilde at a time!

Dear Reader,

Welcome back to Manhattan and book two of Wilde Hearts. Thank you so much for reading!

How to Romance a Runaway Bride is the second book of this series, but each one can be read as a stand-alone, so if you missed the first one, don't worry.

This is the story of Zander Wilde and Allegra Clark, childhood friends who made a bargain to marry each other if both of them were still single by the time they turned thirty. Things get a little complicated when one of them appears to have forgotten their agreement.

How to Romance a Runaway Bride was such fun to write. It's a friends-to-lovers story with an emotional twist. It's also an exploration of how the characters see events from the past from two completely different perspectives. Zander and Allegra know one another better and more deeply than anyone else ever could, but when they come together at the beginning of the book, they're strangers. Everything has changed.

Or has it?

If you enjoy *How to Romance a Runaway Bride*, be sure to check out the next book in the Wilde Hearts series—*The Bachelor's Baby Surprise*, coming next month from Special Edition. And if you missed book one of Wilde Hearts, *The Ballerina's Secret*, it's still available wherever books are sold.

Happy reading,

Teri Wilson

How to Romance a Runaway Bride

Teri Wilson

ISBN-13: 978-1-335-46586-3

How to Romance a Runaway Bride

This edition published by arrangement with Harlequin Books S.A.

For questions and comments about the quality of this book, please contact us at CustomerService@Harlequin.com.

Printed in U.S.A.

Teri Wilson is a novelist for Harlequin. She is the author of *Unleashing Mr. Darcy*, now a Hallmark Channel Original Movie. Teri is also a contributing writer at HelloGiggles.com, a lifestyle and entertainment website founded by Zooey Deschanel that is now part of the *People* magazine, *TIME* magazine and *Entertainment Weekly* family. Teri loves books, travel, animals and dancing every day. Visit Teri at teriwilson.net or on Twitter, @teriwilsonauthr.

Books by Teri Wilson

Harlequin Special Edition

Wilde Hearts

The Ballerina's Secret

Drake Diamonds

His Ballerina Bride
The Princess Problem
It Started with a Diamond

HQN Books

Unmasking Juliet
Unleashing Mr. Darcy

For my friends and fellow writers in San Antonio Romance Authors, my local RWA chapter.

You all inspire and uplift me every day.

“You dance secretly inside my heart,
where no one else can see.”

Rumi

Chapter One

Zander Wilde was seeing things. It was the only explanation. He was hallucinating. Or having a stroke. Anything. Because the woman in a frothy white wedding gown who'd just burst through the door of his birthday party at the Bennington Hotel couldn't possibly be real. Not when she looked so very much like Allegra had all those years ago.

"Let's make a deal. If neither of us is married by the time we turn thirty, we'll marry each other," Zander had said. "Agreed?"

"Agreed," Allegra had replied.

Zander's throat grew tight. He hadn't thought about that conversation in a long time. A very long time. Unless the past week or so counted. But it was normal to remember such things under the circumstances, wasn't it? He was turning thirty, and that impulsive little arrangement was a childhood memory. Nothing more. Nothing less. It didn't actually mean anything.

Except here she was, almost a decade and a half later, dressed from head to toe in bridal white.

No one else seemed to notice her sudden appearance, so maybe she was indeed a figment of his imagination. Either that, or the party guests had been distracted by the arrival of his enormous birthday cake. With any luck, it was the former.

He tore his gaze away from her and focused instead on the cake sitting on the table in front of him. The blaze from its thirty candles warmed his face. Someone started to sing the lyrics to "Happy Birthday to You"—maybe one of his sisters or another of the Wildes. He didn't even know. He couldn't seem to concentrate on the very real people and the very real celebration going on around him.

He glanced back up. She was still there—the woman in white—looking even more like Allegra. Same honey-colored hair tumbling about her shoulders in waves. Same petite frame. She pressed a hand to her abdomen and took a few deep breaths, nodding to herself the way she'd always done backstage before a dance competition when she was a teenager. Zander had witnessed this private ceremony of nerves on many occasions. He'd just never seen it performed when Allegra looked like she'd recently climbed down from atop a wedding cake.

Zander blinked. Hard. This was one realistic daydream.

He cleared his throat and fixed his attention on the candles melting all over the thick frosting of the chocolate-bourbon masterpiece the hotel's pastry chef had created. The pâtissier had really gone all out. It was just another perk that came with being CEO of one of New York's most legendary hotels, Zander supposed. He forced himself to smile—or tried, at least—and realized the singing had stopped.

"You going to blow those out?" Ryan Wilde asked.

Everyone around the table looked at Zander. His sister Tessa and her fiancé, Julian. His mother, Emily, along with about four dozen or so other party guests. All of Zander's staff and closest friends, including his date, whose name he couldn't quite recall at the moment.

Susan. Or Stacy. Something that began with an *S*. They weren't serious, obviously. Zander's dalliances never were.

And now you're seeing imaginary brides.

He was losing it.

No. No, he wasn't. He was perfectly competent. He was at the peak of his career. Two months ago, *GQ* had named him one of Manhattan's "Top Thirty Under Thirty." He was one of the most eligible bachelors in New York, and he had every intention of staying that way.

The ancient deal he'd made with Allegra was messing with his head, that's all. Which was more than a little irritating. Not to mention absurd on every level. Zander hadn't set eyes on Allegra Clark in over a decade, and he was certain it had been even longer than that since she'd given him a passing thought. She'd left Manhattan without even saying goodbye.

Enough reminiscing. Some things were best left

forgotten, and whatever had—or more accurately, *hadn't*—gone on between him and Allegra was definitely one of those things. He squeezed his eyes shut, took a deep breath and readied himself to blow out his candles. In the second before he exhaled, he heard something. A voice from his past, as breathy and velvety soft as he remembered.

"Oh, my," the voice said.

Zander looked up.

"It seems I'm interrupting something." The woman standing with her back pressed to the ballroom door offered a tentative smile. "I'm sorry."

Allegra Clark. Not a figment of his overactive imagination, but real. As real as her floor-length white gown and the bouquet of blush-pink roses in her hand.

Zander opened his mouth to say something, but he couldn't seem to form words. What in the hell was going on?

"It's nothing. Just a little birthday party," Zander's mother said. She shot a questioning glance at Zander and he stared back at her, paralyzed by shock.

Emily cleared her throat. "Join us. The more the merrier, and all that."

She jumped up from her chair, scurried toward Allegra and gathered her into a welcoming hug. His sister Chloe followed suit, and Zander began to wonder if anyone was going to mention Allegra's unusual attire or if they were going to keep pretending anything about this scenario was remotely normal.

"Thank you," Allegra said. She cast a panicked glance at the closed door behind her. Then her chin wobbled in a way that brought about a sudden, intense ache in Zander's chest.

He looked past Allegra, hoping with every fiber of his being that there was a groom standing somewhere nearby. Surely there was.

No such luck. There was no husband, apparently. A growing sense of panic welled in Zander's chest, which did nothing to improve his mood. He'd single-handedly restored the Bennington Hotel to its glory days. He was one of the most powerful CEOs in the city. He could snap his fingers and in an instant, a team of security officers would materialize and discreetly escort Allegra from the building. Under no circumstances should he be losing his cool over the sight of a woman in a wedding gown.

But this wasn't just any woman.

"Hey." Beside Zander, Tessa frowned. "Isn't that..."

"Yes. It is." Since Tessa was hearing impaired, Zander signed the words in addition to speaking them in a voice that sounded angrier than he intended.

He actually hadn't realized he was angry. Surprised? Yes. Confused? Absolutely. But angry? At Allegra? He wouldn't have admitted as much back in the day. But he supposed he was. In reality, he'd probably been angry at Allegra for a very long time.

"Allegra Clark. Wow," Tessa muttered. "After all this time."

"Yep," Zander said and drained his glass of Veuve Clicquot. He should probably do something. Or at least speak to her. But he was at a complete loss. He just sat there like an idiot, staring as his other sister and his mother made a big fuss over Allegra. They hurried her over to the bar, oohing and aahing all the way across the expanse of the ballroom.

"Let's get you something to drink. A brandy, perhaps. You seem rattled," his mother said.

Chloe beamed at Allegra. "Isn't that a lovely dress, though? You look beautiful."

She did, actually. Quite beautiful. Far prettier than Zander remembered, which was something of a shock. Even when they'd been at odds, Allegra had never failed to take his breath away.

He could remember with perfect clarity the first time it had happened—a simmering summer evening in early August. He and Allegra couldn't have been older than ten or eleven. They'd taken advantage of her father's place on the board of the Museum of Natural History and spent the day wandering among the dinosaurs in the building's cool air-conditioning. Allegra had been running ahead of him, like she always did, while he struggled to catch up. Then she'd stopped suddenly to turn and say something. For the life of him, he couldn't recall what she'd said. But he remembered everything else about that moment—the swirl of starlight in the windows overhead, the massive T. rex skeleton looming behind her in the darkness, strange and beautiful.

Most of all, he remembered the way his heart had stopped when she'd smiled. It was as if he'd seen her for the very first time, this girl he'd known for as long as he'd been alive.

Allegra's pretty, he'd thought. The realization had struck him like a physical force. He remembered clutching at the front of his T-shirt, not unlike the time a basketball had hit him hard in the back at recess and knocked the wind right out of him.

But they'd been kids back then, Allegra no more than a girl. The woman who'd just interrupted his birthday party was all grown-up, and to Zander's great dismay, she was very possibly the most stunning creature he'd ever set eyes on. She had impossibly full lips, eyes that glittered like sapphires and an arch in her left eyebrow that gave him the impression she'd accumulated more than her fair share of secrets over the course of the past decade.

"What do you suppose she's doing here?" Tessa turned to look at Zander.

Zander coughed and tore his gaze from the long row of tiny white buttons that ran the full length of Allegra's spine, stopping just above the curve of her lush bottom. "How should I know?"

Tessa's gaze narrowed. "Hey, didn't you ask her to marry you once?"

Zander clenched his jaw. "No."

Because he hadn't. Not technically. They'd had a deal. A stupid, childish deal. They'd been thick as thieves back then. Either one of them could have suggested it.

It had been Zander's idea, though.

That much he couldn't deny.

Allegra took the glass one of the women thrust at her and cleared her throat. "Thank you, um…"

Both of the women peering back at her looked familiar.

She took a swig of the amber liquid and nearly

choked. Allegra never drank alcohol straight up. Then again, she'd never run out on a wedding before. Today was a day of firsts, it seemed.

She stared into her glass. "What is this again?"

"Brandy," the older woman said. "Neat."

Allegra let out a snort. *Neat.* What a joke. There was nothing neat about her current situation. She couldn't have made a bigger mess if she'd tried.

She took another swallow, a smaller one this time. Her head spun a little. She was vaguely aware of her bridal bouquet slipping from her grasp and falling onto the ballroom floor with a thud.

The older of the two women bent to pick it up, and when Allegra took in her straight spine and the fluid grace of her movements, reality dawned. "Mrs. Wilde?"

"Yes, dear," she said, and Allegra blinked back tears.

Emily Wilde had been her childhood dance teacher. More than that, really. She'd been Zander's mother. Allegra had spent more time at the Wilde home than she had her own.

Her gaze flitted to the younger woman standing beside Emily. "Chloe, is that you?"

"It is." Chloe smiled. "It's so good to see you, Allegra."

What was happening? She hadn't seen any of the Wildes in years, not since she'd left Manhattan. Now here they were, at her wedding.

No. You fled from your wedding, remember?

That's right. Allegra probably shouldn't be drinking on an empty stomach. Emily and Chloe weren't at her wedding. Rather, they were in the room next door at some kind of fancy celebration. Allegra's gaze drifted from one end of the dazzling ballroom to the other. There were people everywhere. In her haste to escape her nuptials, she'd dashed into the first door she'd seen. It led to an adjoining ballroom apparently.

She'd crashed a party.

In a wedding dress.

Wonderful.

Allegra closed her eyes and took another fortifying gulp of her brandy. Somewhere close by, a throat cleared. A very masculine throat.

She opened her eyes and found a dashing man dressed in what could only be called a power suit parting the crowd and charging straight toward her with a few hotel staff members trailing behind him. Everything about the man exuded confidence, from his peaked lapels and slicked-back hair to the bold Windsor knot in his tie. But beneath his arrogant exterior, there was something undeniably familiar.

Allegra's knees went wobbly.

Zander. Zander Wilde. *Her* Zander.

Not that he'd ever actually been hers. They'd never dated or anything. He hadn't taken her to prom or the homecoming dance. They'd just been friends. Best friends. And for some reason, that had made Allegra feel even closer to him than if she'd been his girlfriend. Girlfriends came and went. Zander had *known* her.

But that was yesterday. Now she could only stand there and try to make sense of the fact that he was wearing a three-piece suit just like the one her father had always worn. She couldn't quite wrap her head around it. Not one bit. And he looked so…so…*serious.* Angry, even.

Allegra cast a glance over her shoulder in search of the object of his wrath, but there was no one there. She swiveled to face Zander again. Sure enough, his glare appeared to be aimed directly at her.

Her heart started pounding again. Her tummy did a little flip. But she didn't feel panicky. No, this was something different. Something not as frightening as a panic attack. In fact, it almost felt like attraction.

Odd.

And wrong. So very wrong. This was Zander. Her friend. Or at least he'd *been* her friend. Now he was just…nothing. And Allegra was still wearing the dress she'd chosen to wear to her wedding. *To another man.* So there was nothing remotely appropriate about the butterflies swarming in her belly.

She swallowed and decided they weren't butterflies at all. She was overwhelmed. Period. It had been quite a day. A lump formed in her throat, and she suddenly had to blink back tears.

Zander came to a stop directly in front of her. A furious knot tensed in his jaw. His very square, very manly jaw. Zander Wilde had done quite a bit of growing up since she'd seen him last.

"Allegra." He gave her a businesslike nod, as if she was a total stranger.

Why on earth was he acting so ridiculous?

"Zander." She threw her arms around him in a bear hug. Maybe it was a little presumptuous since they hadn't seen each other in so many years. But gosh, it was good to see him. Better than she would ever have imagined. The lump in her throat grew threefold.

Zander stiffened and promptly peeled her arms away

from him. “Could everyone let us have a word for a minute, please? In private.”

Chloe smiled at Allegra over Zander’s shoulder, then wandered to the far side of the ballroom along with the others. Emily, however, lingered.

Zander seemed to sense her presence. “You, too, Mom.”

She shook her head. “Zander, maybe you should—”

“Mom, please. This is between Allegra and me.” For a split second, his steely gaze grew soft. Allegra caught a brief glimpse of the boy she’d once known. Then before she could even smile at him, he was gone. “No one else.”

“Fine.” Emily glared at the back of her son’s head, then aimed a parting smile at Allegra. “It’s nice to see you again, dear. You look gorgeous. Such a beautiful bride.”

Bride. Oh, goodness.

In her shock at seeing Zander again, she’d forgotten all about her dress. He clearly hadn’t. The way he was staring, she might think Zander Wilde had never seen a woman in a wedding gown before.

“What was that all about? Clearing the room.” She glanced at the hotel staff nervously hovering just a few yards away. “Are those your minions? Are you going to have them escort me off the property or something?”

Allegra laughed.

Zander didn’t. Not even close. “Those are my employees. I’m the CEO of this hotel. No one is going to escort you off the property, but come on, Allegra. You can't be serious right now. What are you doing here? And why on earth are you wearing *that*?"

He waved a hand at her gown, but didn't seem to look directly at it. In fact, he appeared to avoid looking directly at her altogether and instead focused on a spot somewhere above her head.

This was getting more annoying by the minute. She'd just bailed on her wedding. She was mentally, emotionally and physically exhausted. She needed a nap and a good long cry. *Not* an argument. Especially an argument that had somehow started without her.

"I'll tell you why I'm wearing this as soon as you explain why you're being such a jerk. You used to be nice." She had no intention of confiding in him. Frankly, she couldn't think of a more humiliating idea. And she didn't want to cry in front of him, but bitter tears were already stinging her eyes. A sob caught in the back of her throat.

She should be married right now, but here she was. Alone. Just like always.

How had everything gone so horribly wrong?

She looked Zander up and down, from the top of his perfectly groomed head to the tips of his wing tip–clad toes. She wished he wasn't so good-looking. It made his new, smug attitude much more annoying. "What exactly is going on here?"

Zander's gaze narrowed. He crossed his arms over his chest, and Allegra pretended not to notice how much broader that chest had gotten since eleventh grade.

"What's going on is my birthday party. My *thirtieth* birthday," he said with a tone that implied she should have known.

Ten years ago, maybe even five, she would have. But Allegra had spent more than a decade trying so hard to eradicate bad memories that some of the good ones slipped through the cracks. The bad ones never did.

Her gaze strayed toward the birthday cake on the table in the center of the room. She'd run out on a wedding and crashed her oldest friend's birthday party all on the same day. And if the woman standing beside the cake looking slightly forlorn was any indication, she'd also interrupted Zander on a date.

"I'm sorry if I've ruined your party. Happy birthday." She swallowed. Something still didn't seem quite right. Why would Zander, who so clearly had grown into an adult man, be so upset about a birthday party?

She didn't care. This painful little reunion was over. Allegra had more important things to worry about—things like picking up the shattered pieces of her life. Again.

She gathered her billowing skirt in her hands and moved in the direction of the ballroom's grand double doors. With any luck, she could somehow make it to the hotel's registration desk without bumping into any of her wedding guests. Or, heaven forbid, the press. "I'll just get a room and—"

Zander cut her off. "Stop, Allegra. This isn't happening."

"What's not happening?" Ugh, was the hotel full? Couldn't Mr. Hotshot CEO pull some strings and get her a room?

She hated to ask him for a favor, especially when he was looking at her like he'd love nothing more than to turn her out on the street in her Vera Wang. But there were reporters outside. She needed a room. And she really, really needed to get out of her wedding dress and into something else. *Anything* else. Pronto.

"This. Us." Zander inhaled a deep, measured breath. Then he *finally* looked at her. Really looked. Allegra almost wished he hadn't, because these weren't the same eyes she remembered from her childhood, full of innocence and hope. She didn't know the man who belonged to these eyes. "I won't marry you, Allegra. Not now. Not ever."

Chapter Two

Zander crossed his arms and told himself he'd done absolutely nothing wrong, despite the glare his mother was currently aiming at him from across the ballroom. He'd probably get an earful from her later on. Emily Wilde was no shrinking violet. She was a woman with strong opinions and a tendency to meddle, and now that Zander's younger sister was happily engaged as well as dancing with a major ballet company, Emily no longer felt the need to hover over Tessa. The family matriarch had moved on to Zander's personal life instead.

Oh, joy.

She wanted him married. She wanted grandchildren, preferably a boy, who could ensure that the Wilde family name and legacy would live on long after she was gone. Thus she made Zander curse his status as the only male offspring on a regular basis. He'd just as soon let some other guy get married and carry on the family name. Except there wasn't another guy. Just him, a fact that was all the more painfully obvious now that he had a bride standing in front of him.

I won't marry you, Allegra. Not now. Not ever.

Granted, it might have sounded a bit harsh, but he'd only said what needed to be said, plain and simple. Emily would no doubt accuse him of causing a scene, which was absurd. If anyone was causing a scene, it was Allegra.

She'd crashed his birthday party. *In a wedding gown.* Had she honestly expected him to just run off into the sunset and marry her? Had she gone insane since she'd left town?

She peered up at him, lush lips pressed together and a cute little wrinkle in her forehead. She didn't look crazy. She looked confused. Confused and undeniably gorgeous. Looking into her luminous blue eyes made Zander's chest hurt for some strange reason. He focused once again on the sparkling chandelier hanging over her head. That dress…those eyes—it was all too much.

"*Marry* me?" Her voice rang with incredulity. And if Zander wasn't mistaken, a fair amount of amusement.

He lifted an eyebrow. *You're the one in a wedding dress, sweetheart.*

"You can't be serious," she said, deadpan.

Zander didn't say a word, but simply held her gaze. He'd said his piece. There was no way he'd be held to a silly promise he'd made as a kid. Now she just needed to go back to wherever she'd come from before she embarrassed herself further.

Allegra's gaze narrowed, as if she was trying to peer

inside his head. Then her pretty pink lips curved into a grin. She was smiling? Now?

Maybe she really was unstable. The poor thing.

Zander reached for her hand. A mistake. A huge one. A long time ago, he'd read something in a magazine article that said a simple touch could possess memory, a notion he'd dismissed as sentimental nonsense. Memories lived in the realm of the mind. They were made up of thoughts, images and unflinching emotions. How could a person's flesh be capable of such complexities?

But the moment his fingertips connected with Allegra's, something strange happened. His limbs felt looser all of a sudden, and his spirit lifted. He remembered the soaring sensation of holding Allegra in his arms and twirling across the dance floor. He remembered ice-skating in Central Park, a lacy veil of snow in Allegra's hair and his heart pounding hard in a darkened museum. He felt like a kid again. It was like being knocked flat by a New York blizzard.

He dropped her hand and recrossed his arms. Revisiting the past had no place on his current agenda. She needed help. Obviously. He should call someone, but who? She no longer had any family in New York.

Did she have any family left at all? Anywhere?

"Look, Allegra—" he began.

She cut him off. "You seriously think I'm here because I want to marry you?"

She let out a giggle, then appeared to make a feeble attempt to keep her mouth shut. It was no use. Another giggle escaped, louder this time, until she was quite literally laughing in his face.

Allegra's laugh hadn't changed a bit. Once upon a time, it had been one of Zander's favorite sounds. Not anymore. "You find the idea of marrying me amusing, do you?"

"Actually…" She cleared her throat and managed to collect herself. For the most part. There was still far too much snickering going on for his taste. "I do."

"'I do.'" Zander lifted an eyebrow. "You even sound like a bride."

That managed to stop her snickering. "Oh, get over yourself. I haven't even seen you in thirteen years."

Actually, it was closer to fourteen. Not that Zander was counting. He clenched his jaw to keep himself from opening his mouth and saying it out loud.

Allegra's smile faded. "You're serious, aren't you? You actually think I came here after all this time to drag you to the altar. Tell me, Mr. Suit, what kind of evidence do you have to support this delusion?"

Mr. Suit.

Her voice dripped with disdain. Zander probably should have expected that. He hadn't. Then again, everything about this insane night was coming out of left field. *Happy birthday to me.*

"You mean other than your attire?" He ordered himself not to look at the dress again. But then he fixed his gaze on the delicate row of tiny shimmering crystals that ran along the curves of her shoulders.

"Circumstantial evidence," she said, sounding like the lawyer's daughter she'd been. Then she shrugged, and those glittering crystals dazzled beneath the soft light of the chandelier. "You're going to have to do better than that. Who says what I'm wearing has anything to do with you?"

"*We* did. You and me. Fourteen years ago."

He waited for her expression to betray her resistance, for a hint of what had transpired between them so long ago to show on her porcelain face. They'd loved one another once. Not romantic love, but something quite different. Something deeper.

Or so he'd thought.

She blinked but kept on looking at him like he was the one who was acting nuts. "I don't know what in the world you're talking about."

He had to give her credit. She was doing a good job of feigning innocence. A great job, actually.

Zander took a step closer. He didn't want to humiliate her in front of Manhattan's glittering elite. He just wanted to put a stop to things once and for all. If he was being honest, he also wanted her to leave. The sooner the better.

He'd grown accustomed to life without her. Things were simpler now. Rational. Predictable. Sure, it had been hard at first. There had been times when he'd closed his eyes and still seen her wild thicket of dark hair and those legs that seemed to go on forever as she struck a ballroom-dance pose. And maybe the warm vanilla scent of her perfume had lingered on his favorite sweatshirt for a time after she'd gone. But eventually it had faded away.

As had his questions.

Why had she left without saying goodbye? Why hadn't she ever come back, even for a visit?

Had she missed him the way he'd missed her?

He didn't want to ask those questions anymore, but if she stayed too long, he would. He knew he would. And he wasn't altogether sure he'd like the answers.

After the accident, she'd gone to live with her aunt in Cambridge. That much he knew. But Boston was just a train ride away. He'd never for a moment suspected she'd gone away for good.

Zander lowered his voice. "You can stop pretending, Allegra. We both know the truth. You're here because of our deal."

She frowned. "What deal?"

If Zander hadn't known better, he'd have thought she'd actually forgotten. But that wasn't possible. Was it?

Of course not.

Still, her acting skills had improved since her disastrous audition for the eighth-grade play. She'd cried in Zander's arms for hours after school that day.

He swallowed. "The deal we made to marry one another if we were still unattached by our thirtieth birthdays."

"Oh." She shook her head. "I'm afraid I don't remember that at all."

Zander stared. If Guy Lombardo's orchestra had appeared out of nowhere and begun to play "Happy Birthday to You," he'd have been less surprised. She wasn't here because of their deal. She didn't even remember it.

Unbelievable.

"Are you sure you didn't have that arrangement with somebody else? Gretchen Williams, maybe?" Allegra said.

"Gretchen Williams?" She couldn't be serious. He'd gone out with Gretchen exactly three times, and that had been three times too many. Besides, the last he'd heard, Gretchen had moved to Connecticut and had five kids. She hadn't needed a backup plan. "Absolutely not. It was you."

It was always you.

Zander's temples throbbed. He needed to get out of here.

But this was his place of business. He practically lived here. Disappearing wasn't an option. Besides, wasn't that Allegra's specialty?

"I see." Allegra's voice went soft, and she looked at him for a long silent moment. And somehow the silence between them seemed more truthful than anything they'd yet to say to one another.

Zander had the sudden urge to reach for her, to pull her into his arms and greet her the way he should have the moment she'd walked through the door. When she'd gone away all those years ago, her absence had just about killed him. He'd missed her, damn it. He still did, even after all this time.

Then Zander's cousin Ryan appeared at his side. The fact that Ryan was wearing his serious hotel-management face rather than his party-going-family-member face ensured that whatever sentimental moment Zander and Allegra might be on the verge of sharing was officially ruined.

Ryan cleared his throat. "Zander, I hate to interrupt. But we've got a problem. A big one."

"Right." Zander nodded. He couldn't decide if he should curse the interruption or be grateful for it. He gave Allegra a tight smile. "It was good to see you again. My apologies for the misunderstanding."

Then he turned his back on Allegra Clark without waiting for an explanation or even a goodbye. After all, parting words had never been their strong suit.

The sight of Zander's retreating pinstripes jarred something loose inside Allegra. Something that almost made her knees buckle. Something that made her feel dangerously close to coming apart at the seams.

She took a deep breath and counted to ten as she watched him walk away. He murmured something to the man beside him, strode past the untouched cake and disappeared through the ballroom's gilded double doors.

He'd walked right out of his own birthday party without so much as an apology. Or even an explanation.

Typical suit.

Allegra couldn't remember any of her own birthday parties that hadn't been interrupted in a similar fashion. Until she'd turned sixteen, obviously. On her sweet sixteen, she would have given anything to have her father there, kissing her cheek as he dashed off to some kind of work emergency.

Her throat grew tight. She squared her shoulders, slipped out of the ballroom and marched toward the registration desk. She'd managed to walk out on her own wedding today without shedding a tear. She would *not* let a brief encounter with Zander Wilde reduce her to a weepy mess.

Anyway, she was perfectly fine. She'd just been rattled to see him after so many years, which was totally normal. There was nothing to be emotional about at all as far as Zander was concerned.

Except that he thought you'd come back to marry him, of all things.

"Can I help you?" The young man behind the registration desk beamed at her. "Let me guess—you're checking into the honeymoon suite?"

"Um, no." She shuddered. "Definitely not."

"Oh." He glanced at her dress. Allegra couldn't wait

to take off the horrid thing. She just wanted to wrap herself up in one of the hotel's thick terry-cloth robes, climb into bed and sleep for a while. A century, maybe.

"Well, uh, how can I assist you, then?"

"I just need a room." Before he could ask, she added, "A single, not a double."

He frowned. "For just one person?"

Allegra sighed. Mightily. "Yes."

He nodded but still managed to look utterly perplexed. Too bad. "May I ask the name on the reservation?"

"I don't have one."

"No reservation?" His frown deepened. "I'm sorry, but we don't have any single rooms available without a reservation."

This day kept getting better and better. "Fine. I'll take a double."

But the desk clerk wasn't any more accommodating. "I'm afraid we don't have any double rooms available either."

Allegra's heart started beating hard again. This couldn't be happening.

"Fine. I'll take the honeymoon suite." Desperate times called for desperate measures, and these were indeed desperate times.

The hotel clerk shrugged. He was really beginning to get on Allegra's nerves. "That room is booked, as well. We're completely full. Without a reservation, I'm afraid I can't help you."

"Full? *Full?* As in there's not a room of any kind available?" It couldn't be true. Where on earth would she go? What was she supposed to do? Go marching back into her wedding to ask her erstwhile fiancé for a ride to the airport?

Even if the hotel clerk took pity on her and came up with a room, she had no way to pay for it. She'd walked out of the ceremony with nothing but her bridal bouquet. She wasn't even sure where her purse—and her wallet full of credit cards—was at the moment.

Why had she agreed to get married in Manhattan?

She should have insisted on a nice, simple ceremony in Cambridge, where she and Spencer actually lived. How had she let herself get talked into coming back here?

Because Spencer was a politician, that's why. He'd wanted a big, splashy wedding, one that would look good in all the newspapers. A grand show. Allegra just hadn't realized she was nothing but a prop.

How could she have been so monumentally stupid?

"We're completely booked." The clerk gave her a sympathetic smile, and something inside Allegra died just a little. "Can I do anything else for you? Call a car, perhaps?"

Behind her, someone chimed in. "That won't be necessary."

Allegra spun around and found herself face-to-face with Zander's mother. Emily Wilde wasn't exactly the first person she wanted to chat with after the oddly uncomfortable encounter she'd just had with Zander. But it was definitely preferable to talking to Zander himself. "Mrs. Wilde, hello."

"Since when do you call me Mrs. Wilde? I'm Emily, remember?" The older woman gave her a warm smile. "I didn't mean to eavesdrop. I was just on my way out since it seems the birthday party has ended, and I overheard."

"I was trying to get a room, but it seems the hotel is booked."

"Winter in New York is always a busy time of year. But, of course, you know that." Emily tilted her head. "Isn't your birthday right around the corner? I seem to remember it being during the snowy season."

Indeed it was. Just two weeks away. Allegra's thirtieth, which meant if she'd ever made that ancient deal with Zander, they still had fourteen days to make good on it. Not that they'd made any such arrangement. And not that she'd ever in a million years marry the man.

When had he turned into such a grump? And what was he doing running a hotel? The Zander she knew wanted to run the family business someday. The Wilde School of Dance. She'd have been less surprised to see him starring in a Broadway play than strutting around wearing a business suit, surrounded by minions.

Zander Wilde's profession should be the least of your worries at the moment. You're homeless, and the only article of clothing you own is a wedding gown.

"Allegra, you don't look well." Emily pressed a hand to Allegra's forehead. "You need to lie down, dear."

Allegra nodded. Emily was right. She'd never needed to rest so much in her life. She felt like she'd been running for the better part of fourteen years. In a way, she supposed she had. But it wasn't as if she could just curl up on the sofa in the hotel lobby.

Could she?

No, of course she couldn't. She'd probably get in

trouble. Or even arrested. She let out a hysterical laugh. Wouldn't that be the perfect ending to this horrible day? To have Zander call the cops on her.

Zander Wilde, who thought she'd been pining away for him since the day she'd left town.

"You'll stay with me," Emily said as matter-of-factly as if she'd just offered Allegra a stick of gum rather than a roof over her head.

"What?" Allegra shook her head. "Oh, no, I couldn't..."

But Emily had already removed her coat and was wrapping it around Allegra's shoulders as she led her toward the revolving door. "Of course you can. How many afternoons did you come home with us after dance class when you were a girl?"

More than Allegra could count. "But things are different now." She slowed to a stop two feet from the exit. "Emily, I can't. I'm afraid that might upset Zander. We had a disagreement a few minutes ago."

"I heard." Emily nodded. "Half of Manhattan heard, actually."

Fabulous. Just fabulous.

"It doesn't matter what Zander thinks. It's my house, not his." Emily gave Allegra's waist a gentle squeeze. "And if you don't mind my saying, it doesn't really look like you have a lot of options."

She didn't. Zero, in fact.

"Allegra, dear. I can't leave you here all alone. I owe it to your mom and dad to see that you're taken care of." Emily's voice dropped to a whisper. "Come on home."

At the mention of her parents, the last shreds of Allegra's resistance crumbled. She didn't have the strength to fight the past. Not tonight. Not now.

Come on home.

She wanted nothing more than to go home, if only she knew how to get there.

Chapter Three

Zander stared at Ryan sitting in one of the wingback chairs opposite his desk and tried to wrap his mind around the bomb his cousin had just dropped. "A reporter called here to ask whether or not the hotel has been *cursed*?"

This was a first. Zander was no stranger to New York's tabloid press. He was fully aware of how brutal it could be. But a curse? That seemed beyond ridiculous, even for a rag like the *Post* or the *Daily News*.

"She wasn't asking exactly." Ryan frowned. "She's going to run with it."

Zander released a tense exhale. He didn't need this kind of complication. Today of all days. He was still a little rattled after his encounter with Allegra. *A lot* rattled, frankly. Mainly by her assertion that she didn't even remember their marriage pact.

Then why the wedding gown?

"Fine." He needed a drink. A *real* drink. No more birthday champagne. A martini, maybe. Something potent enough to eradicate the memory of the past half hour of his life, if such a drink existed. "A single negative tabloid article won't kill us, even one that says we're cursed. At least they get points for creativity."

He waited for the pained look on Ryan's face to relax a little.

It didn't. If anything, the crease between his cousin's brows deepened.

"It's not a tabloid," Ryan said. Then he uttered the only three words powerful enough to tear Zander's thoughts away from Allegra Clark dressed in bridal white tulle. "It's the *Times*."

This had to be a bad joke. The *New York Times* had won more Pulitzer Prizes than any other paper in the world. "Good one. You almost had me. But the Gray Lady is a New York institution. It's a serious publication. They'd never run a story about a hotel being cursed."

"Think again." Ryan lifted a sardonic eyebrow. "The Society section would."

Zander swallowed, longing once again for the smooth burn of vodka, vermouth and a little olive brine sliding down his throat. Things were apparently worse than he'd anticipated.

The *Times*, for God's sake. Only the society page, but still…

It wasn't *just* the society page, though, as Zander soon realized.

Ryan took a deep breath and lowered the boom. "Specifically, the Vows column."

Zander clenched his gut. "The Vows column? From the Sunday Wedding section?"

"The one and only." Ryan sighed.

Having the hotel lambasted on the front page would have been better than the Vows column announcing that the Bennington was cursed. People all over the damn world read the wedding announcements in the Sunday edition of the *Times*. Like every other luxury hotel in Manhattan, a sizable portion of the Bennington's business came from the wedding industry. Moonstruck brides and grooms.

He shook his head. This couldn't happen. Not after he'd worked so hard to restore the Bennington to its former glory. "I don't understand where this is coming from. Why would a columnist from Vows think we're cursed?"

Ryan frowned. "You seriously have to ask?"

"I do, actually."

I do.

The instant the words left his mouth, he remembered Allegra saying the same thing while she stood in front of him, looking like she'd just walked out of a fairy tale.

He'd taunted her. *You even sound like a bride.*

Now reality was finally coming together with horrific clarity.

Damn. He groaned. "We've had another runaway bride, haven't we?"

"Bingo." Ryan seemed to be fighting a smirk. "The bride who crashed your birthday party just now was the latest. You know, the one you assumed was here to strong-arm you into marrying her."

"Yeah, I get that." *Now* he did, anyway.

Zander sighed. No wonder Allegra had laughed in

his face. She hadn't turned up to make good on their deal. She'd been on the run from her own wedding to a completely different man.

Perhaps he shouldn't have jumped to conclusions. But the timing seemed awfully fortuitous. It wasn't as if he'd *wanted* to believe she'd come back for him.

You sure about that?

Beneath the surface of his desk, Zander's hands curled into fists. Of course he was sure.

Ryan's gaze narrowed. "What's the story there, if you don't mind my asking? The two of you were engaged once?"

"No," Zander said with a little too much force. Then, more evenly, he added, "It wasn't like that."

Ryan stared blankly at him, waiting for more.

Zander was in no mood to oblige. "Back to the matter at hand. We have two weddings on the schedule this weekend. Which one just went belly-up?"

Zander didn't personally handle the hotel's wedding-planning details, but as with everything else that went on beneath the roof of the fabled building, he supervised with a watchful eye. It was his job to know what was going on, and he definitely would have noticed if they'd had a wedding on the schedule with a bride named Allegra Clark.

Ryan took a beat too long to answer. "The big one. The Warren wedding."

The Warren wedding, as in Spencer Warren, city councilman and mayoral candidate for the city of Cambridge, Massachusetts. No wonder the *Times* had already taken notice.

The hotel roster had listed the bride's name as Ali Clark. So Allegra was going by Ali now?

Zander wasn't sure what he found more surprising—the fact that Allegra had changed her name or that she'd ever considered being a politician's wife.

It was time to face the facts. He no longer knew her. Allegra was a stranger now. She wasn't even Allegra anymore, and she didn't want to marry him any more than he wanted to marry her.

He also had far more pressing matters to deal with at the moment. "This is our third runaway bride in the span of a month."

Ryan nodded. "We also had one about twelve weeks ago."

No wonder the *Times* thought the Bennington was cursed. "Once the Vows column goes forward, no one will want to book a wedding here."

"We're screwed," Ryan said.

"No, we're not." Zander gave his head a slow, methodical shake. "We'll just have to prove them wrong."

He wasn't going down without a fight. He'd worked too long and too hard to let a runaway bride bring him to his knees.

Even a runaway bride he'd once been foolish enough to love.

Allegra woke the next morning when the first rays of soft pink sunlight peeked through the ruffled curtains of Emily Wilde's guest room. Her first conscious thought was how pretty the cozy attic space looked, with its white barrel-vaulted ceiling and antique pedestal sink in the corner. Her second conscious thought was that she couldn't remember the last time she'd had such a good night's sleep.

It defied logic. She was homeless, for all practical

purposes. Stuck in New York with no belongings, no job and no fiancé. No plan. Yet, she felt more at peace than she had in months. Maybe she'd actually done the right thing, for once. She'd made a good choice in coming back…coming home.

Except this wasn't home. This was Zander's mother's house. His mother's room. The pale gray flannel pajamas Allegra had slept in didn't belong to her either. They were at least three sizes too big. She could only guess they'd once belonged to Zander's father.

Still, it felt nice here. Peaceful. She peeled back the curtain and watched the snow float down from the sky. Slowly, softly, like feathers shaken loose from a pillow. A tiny black kitten tiptoed its way through the white fluff on the sidewalk down below. Everything was so picturesque that Allegra's heart gave a little lurch.

Don't get used to it. You can't stay here. You cannot.

Except where else could she go?

Somehow she'd thought she could figure it all out after she got some sleep. But nothing had changed. Not really. The hotel was booked. Even if they'd had a room and even if she'd managed to locate her purse, her debit card would have only been good for two or three nights. Four at the most. She'd spent every last dime on her dream wedding. There'd been the fancy caterer, the string quartet, the flowers…

An image of her extravagant bridal bouquet falling to the floor of the Bennington Hotel's ballroom flashed through Allegra's mind. She squeezed her eyes closed.

Everything is going to be okay. It will.

But when she opened her eyes, she found herself looking at a pouf of tulle at the foot of the bed. Her discarded wedding dress.

Everything was not okay.

She tossed aside the sheets, climbed out of bed and headed down the curved, Victorian-style staircase to Emily's kitchen. She needed coffee. A gallon of it, if possible.

"Good morning, dear. How did you sleep?" Emily sat at the kitchen table and looked up from the copy of the *New York Times* in her hands.

Allegra glanced at the front page. She spotted Spencer's name in a headline just below the fold and pointedly averted her gaze.

"I slept great, thank you." Allegra looked around the kitchen, with its blue-and-white-toile wallpaper and shelves crammed full of mismatched china teacups. It hadn't changed a bit since the last time she'd stood in this spot.

"Come sit down." Emily folded the newspaper closed. "I've got your breakfast warming in the oven."

"You didn't need to do that, Mrs. Wilde. Honestly, you've done enough."

"Nonsense." Emily planted her hands on Allegra's shoulders and steered her toward the table. "And stop calling me Mrs. Wilde. We're not in dance class. Besides, I've known you since you were so tiny that your head didn't even reach the top of the ballet barre."

Allegra sat and watched as the older woman removed a breakfast casserole from the oven that looked big enough to feed an army. Just how hungry did Emily think she looked?

"Here you go. Dig in while I get you some coffee." Emily slid a plate in front of her.

Allegra couldn't remember the last time someone had cooked her breakfast. Or any meal, for that matter. She could get used to this kind of royal treatment if she stayed here for any length of time.

Which she most definitely would not.

She shouldn't. She couldn't. "This is delicious. Thank you so much. For everything. I'm not sure what I would have done last night if you hadn't offered me your guest room."

"You were in a bit of a pickle," Emily said.

The understatement of the century. Allegra's stomach churned. She set down her fork and forced herself to meet Emily's penetrating gaze.

"Do you want to talk about it?" she asked.

Maybe.

No, actually. She didn't. Not yet, and not with Zander's mother. It was too soon and far too humiliating. "His name is Spencer Warren. But I'm guessing you know that by now."

Allegra glanced at the folded newspaper and her throat grew tight. Her hands started to shake, and she had to remind herself to take a breath.

Not another panic attack. Not now.

"I've made such a mess of things," she whispered.

"I'm sure you did the right thing," Emily said, and even though Allegra knew she was just saying it to be kind, it still made her feel a little better. "You can stay here as long as you wish."

"I can't." It was just too awkward. What would Zander say when he found out she was staying with his mother? A lot, probably. A whole lot.

"Of course you can. I'd love to have someone to dote on."

"But I need to get my life in order." Starting with a

job. And something to wear. And a place to live. "I'm a mess, Emily."

"Think of it as temporary, just until you get your feet under you. A month."

"A *month*?" How many times would she run into Zander if she was living at his mother's house for thirty days? Too many. "Absolutely not."

Emily shrugged. "A week, then. Allegra, I hate to break it to you, but you can't reinvent yourself in one day."

She had a point.

And a week might not be too terrible. How often could Zander come by in seven measly days? He was a CEO now. He probably spent all his waking hours at his fancy hotel. He couldn't even make it through a whole birthday party without working, which was a pretty good indication that he didn't have time to hang around his mother's brownstone. Plus seven days would give her time to come up with some sort of plan.

Still, something about this didn't feel right.

You don't have a choice. Be grateful.

She took a deep breath. "I'll stay a week, if you're sure it's no bother."

Emily waved a hand. "Why on earth would it be a bother?"

"Because I think I embarrassed your son last night. He seemed upset." Yet another understatement.

Emily shrugged and sipped her coffee. "He probably had it coming."

Actually he had. The misunderstanding was 100 percent his fault. He'd assumed she'd shown up in a wedding dress to marry him after all this time. What kind of person made such a nonsensical leap?

An egotistical one. One who was pathologically cocky.

One who'd just walked into the kitchen.

Allegra choked on a bite of eggs. "Zander."

He stood staring at her from the threshold while snowflakes swirled around his head. A shiver coursed through her, and he slammed the door behind him.

"Allegra? What are you doing here?" Zander's gaze dropped to her pajamas, then flitted back to her face. His eyes were red, his face wind chapped. He had a serious case of bed head, yet he was still dressed in his suit from the night before. He looked like he hadn't slept a wink since she'd watched him saunter out of his birthday party.

Allegra's head spun a little. Never in her life had she seen such a handsome exhausted man. His shoulders seemed even broader than they'd been just twelve hours ago. It was baffling. And infuriating. She looked down and stared pointedly at her plate.

"She lives here," Emily said.

Zander let out a bitter laugh. "Very funny."

"I'm not joking. Stop being rude to our guest."

Allegra blinked. *Our* guest? What did that mean? Then she remembered the enormity of the breakfast casserole. And the pajamas.

She lost her grip on her fork and it clattered to the table. She ignored it and fixed her gaze on Zander as the mortifying reality of the situation dawned. "Wait a minute. What are *you* doing here?"

"Zander lives here, too," Emily said far too sweetly. "Did I forget to mention that, dear?"

Chapter Four

For the second time in less than twelve hours, Zander couldn't believe what he was seeing.

He blinked. Hard.

But it didn't do any good. When he opened his eyes, Allegra was still sitting at the kitchen table—in *his* chair—with her hair piled on top of her head, staring right back at him. The Princeton coffee mug in her hand—also his—had paused en route to her pillowy lips.

The longer she gawked at him, the looser her grip on the mug became. Zander sighed and reached for it before she spilled coffee all down the front of the pajamas she was wearing, because yes, those were his, too.

The brush of his fingertips against hers as he plucked the mug out of her hand seemed to pull her out of her trance. Wide-eyed, she swiveled her gaze to his mother. "Um, Emily. You did indeed forget to tell me that Zander lives here."

Zander wholeheartedly doubted it had been an innocent omission, mainly because his mother was avoiding looking him in the eye.

As if he didn't already have enough going on in his life without Emily Wilde playing matchmaker. Marvelous.

He took a gulp of coffee, forgetting it was actually Allegra's until her head snapped back in his direction. Her eyes widened, and he took another, more deliberate sip.

His house, his pajamas, his cup, *his* coffee.

Allegra arched a single eyebrow. "You still live with your mother?"

Technically, it was the other way around. He'd purchased the brownstone from his mother three years ago when the dance school first began to have financial troubles. But Allegra could believe whatever she wanted to believe. He didn't want to share personal family matters with her any more than he wanted to share his pajamas.

He shrugged. "It looks that way, doesn't it?"

Then he drained her coffee cup and set it down on the kitchen counter with a thud.

Allegra's gaze flitted to the mug, then back to him. Her cheeks flared pink. "So what's with last night's suit? Is this some of kind of CEO walk of shame?"

Quite the opposite. He'd been working all night, trying to figure out a way to get ahead of the Vows column. But again, Allegra could believe whatever she wanted. Especially since he could have sworn her deepening flush had a distinctly jealous edge.

He didn't want Allegra to be attracted to him. But he didn't particularly hate the idea either, especially since he'd made such an idiot out of himself the night before.

He crossed his arms, giving her a clear, unobstructed view of the unfastened French cuffs of his dress shirt. "I can't help but wonder why you find that idea so unpleasant."

She rolled her eyes, but Zander wasn't buying it. Not this time. "I'm just surprised, that's all. Especially since you seemed so preoccupied with marrying me the last time I saw you."

Emily stifled a laugh.

Zander loved his mother. He really did. But at the moment, she was trying his patience about as much as the reporter from the Vows column.

He narrowed his gaze at her.

Emily cleared her throat. "Allegra, dear. You've got things wrong. Actually—"

"*Actually*, I sleep at the hotel more often than I do here," Zander said. He didn't need his mother to be any more involved with this situation than she already was. He had bigger problems than whatever assumptions Allegra wanted to make about either his living situation or his sex life. And he certainly didn't want to discuss the latter in front of Emily. That would have been about the only way to make this conversation more awkward than it already was.

He cleared his throat. "The Bennington is full at the moment."

"So I heard," Allegra muttered.

"She had nowhere else to go, Zander." Emily looked up at him.

He knew better than to argue, and a part of him

didn't want to. He cared too much about Allegra to turn her out on the street.

But how had she ended up so alone?

Not your problem. You have enough on your plate, remember?

He cleared his throat and changed the subject. "Read anything interesting this morning?"

Emily followed his gaze until she, too, was staring at the folded copy of the *New York Times* on the kitchen table. "So you've seen it."

"Seen what?" Allegra asked.

Emily shook her head. "It's nothing, dear."

"That's not exactly true," Zander said, choosing not to examine why his mother seemed to have chosen sides in the matter.

He flipped through the newspaper until he landed on the Weddings page. His throat went dry as he looked at the headline. He'd already seen it, of course. He and Ryan had stayed up until the early-morning edition was released so they could get a full assessment of the damage.

It was extensive.

Familiar or not, looking at the words splashed below the Vows header still made his gut churn.

Is the Bennington Hotel Cursed?

He spread the paper open beside Allegra's place mat.

"Your hotel is cursed?" She blinked up at him, and for the first time since he'd stumbled upon her sitting at his kitchen table and making herself at home, Zander allowed himself to look at her. Really look.

She was gorgeous in ways that were both foreign

and familiar. How many times had she sat in that same spot? More than he could count. But never like this. Never with years of silence stretching between them. Even in his sleep-deprived state, there was a very real part of him that wanted to pull up a chair and just talk. Talk the way they used to.

He wasn't altogether sure why that wasn't possible. Maybe because her sudden appearance had just thrown a major wrench in his life, businesswise. Or maybe it had something to do with the way he couldn't quite keep his gaze from straying to the enticing swell of her curves beneath his pajamas. Either way, they couldn't just take up where they'd left off. They weren't kids anymore.

He clenched his jaw. "My hotel is not cursed."

"Of course it's not." Emily waved a dismissive hand. "We know that, dear. I don't understand how the *New York Times* could say such a thing."

"I suggest you read the first paragraph." Zander turned toward the coffee maker and refilled the mug in his hand. There wasn't enough coffee in the world for him to deal with the mess he had on his hands.

But when he turned back around and saw the color draining from Allegra's face as she read the article, guilt got the better of him. He set the full cup onto the table in front of her.

She glanced up at him, blue eyes shining bright.

Don't read too much into it, sweetheart. It's just coffee, not an invitation to stay.

Their gazes held until Emily broke the loaded silence. "I hadn't realized there'd been so many runaway brides at the Bennington lately. Zander, why haven't you said anything?"

"It seemed slightly odd, but calling it a curse never

crossed my mind. Probably because I'm a rational person."

Allegra cleared her throat.

Zander glared at her. "I'm very rational."

"I'm sure you are," she said, but he wasn't buying the innocent act. Not for a minute. "Tell me, did you assume all of the other runaway brides wanted to marry you, too? Or just me?"

He clenched his fists to keep himself from scooping her into his arms, carrying her out the door and depositing her into the nearest snowdrift.

"Four runaway brides in the span of a few months *does* seem strange," Emily said.

Great. If his own mom was buying into the Vows nonsense, what chance did he have?

"Until last night, no one seemed to care. Apparently, three runaway brides are acceptable. But not four." He looked pointedly at Allegra. "The fourth one means it's a curse."

Allegra's gaze narrowed, but Zander couldn't help but notice that she wasn't quite looking him in the eye anymore. "That's the dumbest thing I've ever heard. It's completely arbitrary."

"The fact that your groom is rather high-profile wasn't helpful. When a political candidate gets left at the altar, people tend to notice."

Too far.

He knew he'd crossed a line the moment the words left his mouth. The article wasn't Allegra's fault. Not entirely, anyway. He had no right to taunt her about her almost marriage. No right whatsoever, especially given how close he'd once come to tying the knot.

He didn't know why he was acting like such a jerk.

You know exactly why.

Allegra stared down at the newspaper.

Look at me, damn it. Look at me and tell me again that you don't remember.

"I'm sure each and every one of those brides had a perfectly legitimate reason for walking away," she said. Her voice had gone calm, but Zander could see the tremble in her fingertips as her hands twisted in her lap.

He hated himself just a little bit then. But he couldn't stop himself from asking. He wanted to know. He *needed* to know. "I'd love to hear what those reasons were. Seriously, I'm all ears."

It wasn't the time or a place for a heart-to-heart. He was exhausted, her wedding gown was probably still lying in a heap somewhere and they weren't even alone. But he couldn't think straight when she was sitting there looking like that.

So beautiful. So tempting.

So lost.

"Enough." His mother stood. "Zander, you need to get some sleep. You look like a train wreck. Besides, Allegra doesn't have time for the third degree right now. We have to get to work."

Allegra's head snapped up. "Work? Emily, I'm not sure what you mean."

His mother smiled. "The dance studio, dear. Surely you remember."

Zander turned to go. He'd heard enough. Allegra was back in New York. Back in his life. It made sense she'd end up back at the Wilde School of Dance, as well.

It was where she belonged, even after all this time. Once upon a time Zander had belonged there, too. But those days were over.

* * *

Walking into the Wilde School of Dance was as close to going home as Allegra would ever get. It looked exactly the same as it had all those years ago. Same smooth wood floors, same mirrored walls, same old blue record player sitting on the shelf inside the studio where she'd spent the majority of her childhood.

The wave of nostalgia that hit her when she walked through the door nearly knocked her off her feet.

She'd never imagined coming back here again. Ever. But given the choice of either accompanying Emily to the studio or staying back at the brownstone with Zander had been a no-brainer. Still, she purposefully turned her back to the collection of recital photos that lined the wall of the entryway and took a deep breath.

"Why don't you flip through the records and choose some barre music for the adult ballet class?" Emily slipped out of her coat and turned on the computer at the front desk. "You remember where they are, don't you?"

"Sure." Allegra couldn't quite believe Emily's dance school wasn't streaming music for class, but she was happy to have something productive to do. Anything to keep her mind off the last time she'd been in this building.

The record albums were lined up on the shelves beneath the turntable, right where they'd always been. As she flipped through them, she spotted several of her favorites—music that made up the soundtrack to less complicated days, when her biggest concern had been whether or not she'd remember the steps to her competition dance numbers.

She would have given anything to be able to go back to those days.

That was impossible, obviously. She hadn't realized just *how* impossible until she'd spotted Zander staring at her from across the Bennington ballroom.

Her throat grew tight. Why did she keep thinking about him?

Maybe because you're wearing his coat.

Indeed she was. And it smelled magnificent, like cedar and sandalwood. Wholly masculine.

She wiggled her way out of it and tossed it as far as she could throw it. It landed on the chair situated at the front of the room and was now draped over the seat as if Zander himself had just slid it off his broad shoulders.

Allegra's face grew hot. Again.

Enough thinking about Zander Wilde. She might have slept in his pajamas last night, but that didn't mean he had any place in her thoughts. No man did. She was starting over. Alone.

She slid one of the albums from its sleeve, placed it on the turntable and gingerly lowered the needle. The familiar sound of the needle scratching against the record's grooves filled the air. Without thinking about it, Allegra pointed her foot and began sliding it against the polished maple floor in a smooth *rond de jambe.*

"You always did have the best turnout," Emily said.

Allegra moved back into a normal standing position and crossed her arms. "I didn't hear you come in here. I was just messing around."

"Messing around quite beautifully. You've kept up with your technique." Emily winked. "It shows."

Allegra laughed. "You can tell that from one *rond de jambe*?"

"I could tell before you set foot in the studio. I knew the moment I saw you. You carry yourself like a ballerina, dear."

Busted.

Although calling herself a ballerina when she hadn't performed in nearly six months was a stretch. "I danced in the Boston Ballet for a few years. Just the corps de ballet. I wasn't exactly a prima."

Emily shook her head. "Don't do that. Don't undermine yourself. You're clearly talented. You always were. I just always thought you'd become a ballroom dancer."

Allegra's heart gave a little lurch. "Afraid not. I haven't danced ballroom in a long time. Not since..."

She couldn't finish. She didn't need to, though. Emily understood. She'd been the one to give Allegra the news on that rainy New York afternoon fourteen years ago.

There's been an accident, dear. I'm sorry. So, so sorry.

The words echoed in Allegra's consciousness. She remembered them as crisp and clear as if Emily had said them to her yesterday. She remembered the tremor in her voice, the raw devastation in her dance teacher's eyes. More than those things, though, she remembered being wrapped in the tightest embrace of her life. She remembered being held for hours as she'd cried.

Allegra's eyes filled with unshed tears. The voice she remembered so well from that day had been Emily's, but the arms that held her...

Those had been Zander's.

"He stopped dancing then, too, you know," Emily said softly.

Allegra hadn't known. Now that she did, his CEO demeanor made a bit more sense. "He didn't want to start over again with another partner?"

It took time for dance partners to grow accustomed to one another. Months. Sometimes years. Allegra and Zander had never danced with anyone but each other. Even after Allegra had moved to Cambridge to live with her aunt, she couldn't fathom dancing with another partner. So she'd packed away her ballroom shoes and thrown herself into ballet.

"Something like that." Emily's smile didn't quite reach her eyes.

Allegra's gaze strayed over her shoulder, toward the recital photos hanging in matching gold frames.

Don't look. Do. Not.

Her gaze flitted from one picture to the next until she landed on the one of her and Zander in their trademark tango pose—arms wrapped around each other, bodies pressed together tight. One of Allegra's legs was hooked over Zander's hip, and his hand gripped the back of her thigh. She gazed into the camera with a sultry stare, but Zander's attention was focused solely on her.

Something about that captured expression sent a shiver up her spine. The tense set of his jaw and the intensity in his gaze looked uncannily similar to the way he'd been glaring at her since last night.

They'd been pretending back then. They'd simply been teenagers playing dress-up. The seductive moves and the smoldering glances had been for show. Part of a performance.

At least that's what Allegra had told herself at the time.

She cleared her throat, averted her gaze and found Emily watching her intently.

"So it's settled. You'll teach class this morning," the older woman said.

Allegra blinked. "What? No..."

Emily shrugged. "Why not? Do you have other plans for the day?"

She didn't, other than the pressing task of getting her life in order. Which suddenly seemed far too exhausting to contemplate.

"Emily, I've never taught a dance class in my life." She didn't even have a pair of ballet shoes with her. Although the black wraparound dance sweater and leggings that Emily had loaned her for the day suddenly made sense.

"These students are total beginners. All you need to do is a half-hour barre, followed by a very simple adagio combination at center. Add a drawn-out reverence at the end, and boom. You're done. Come to think of it, you could probably handle the beginning children's classes, too."

Allegra shook her head. She was already living with the Wildes. She most definitely didn't need to be working for them, too. "This is a terrible idea."

"It would be a tremendous help. Tessa used to teach this class, but now that she's been promoted to prima at the Manhattan Ballet, she doesn't have time. We have six classes a day here, and I'm afraid I can no longer teach them all myself."

Emily was still teaching? Six classes a day?

Allegra had assumed Emily was retired from teaching. She'd even talked about winding down her teaching career back when Allegra had been a student. The plan had been for Zander's sisters, Tessa and Chloe, to take over the class instruction duties while Emily handled the business end of the school.

From the sound of things, neither one of them had time to teach. Tessa was busy dancing at the Manhattan Ballet, and Chloe was a Rockette. They simply didn't have the time to devote hours every day to the family school.

And Zander had clearly moved on.

Which meant he shouldn't be hanging around the place. That was certainly a plus. Maybe Allegra could help out. Just until she figured out a more permanent plan, obviously.

"This is only temporary. You realize that, right?" She'd committed to a week under Emily's roof. If she taught class for every one of those days maybe she could save up enough money for a new beginning.

It was a start, anyway. Right before the wedding, she'd moved all of her things out of the small apartment in Cambridge she shared with Talia Simms, one of her ballerina friends. Now she was stuck in limbo. Homeless as well as jobless.

She had to start somewhere.

"Just give it a try and see how it goes. Who knows? You might take to it."

She might. She'd always wanted to teach, but she couldn't make a career out of it. Not here. New York was one of the biggest cities in the world. *If* she decided to stay in Manhattan—and she was in no way certain she would—there were plenty of other places where she could teach ballet. She needed to be starting over, not running back to her past.

No matter how tempting the prospect might be.

Her gaze flitted back to the tango photo. Another shiver coursed through her, which she attributed to the whirl of snowflakes floating among the yellow taxicabs just beyond the studio's picture window.

Because it surely didn't have anything to do with Zander Wilde. Not anymore.

"My ballet shoes are back in Cambridge." Her voice sounded raw for some strange reason. Broken.

"No problem. We sell them. I have plenty on hand. I may even have your old dance bag around here somewhere."

Allegra swallowed around the lump that sprang to her throat. "The new ones, please."

She'd spent the past fourteen years refusing to look back, and she wasn't about to start now. Even if there might be more worth remembering than she was willing to admit.

Chapter Five

Zander hadn't planned on returning to the office until he'd gotten at least a few hours of sleep, but that idea ultimately proved fruitless.

Every time he closed his eyes, he saw Allegra looking as comfortable as she could possibly be in his kitchen. In his clothes. In his life.

It was unsettling. More unsettling than seeing her in a wedding gown, if he was being honest with himself. Probably because a very real part of him had enjoyed coming home and finding her there. For a split second he'd even allowed himself to believe she'd been waiting for him.

Then reality had set in.

She hadn't been any more thrilled to see him than he'd been to see her. Perfectly understandable, given the way their little reunion had gone at his birthday party.

But any regrets he had at the way he'd behaved last night had vanished the moment he'd heard about the Vows column. Allegra's sudden reappearance had thrown his life into a tailspin on multiple levels.

And now they were roommates.

"Zander, have you got a minute?" Judging from the weary expression on Ryan's face as he appeared at the entrance to Zander's office, he hadn't gotten much rest either.

"Sure." Zander waved him inside, although he was fairly certain he didn't want to hear whatever news Ryan had come to deliver.

His doubts intensified when Ryan handed him a demitasse cup of espresso before taking a seat.

"Trust me, you're going to want that when I tell you the latest," Ryan said, gesturing toward the white china cup.

Zander took a swallow, relishing the taste of the rich, dark liquid. Bitter, like his mood. "What now?"

How much worse could things possibly get?

"The phone is ringing off the hook." Ryan sank into the chair opposite Zander's desk.

He'd been right. Zander did indeed need the espresso. A gallon of it might have sufficed. "Let me guess. Not one of those callers wanted to reserve the ballroom for a wedding."

Ryan shook his head. "Quite the opposite. We're getting cancellations."

"Cancellations?" Things could get much, much worse than he'd expected. Obviously.

He'd braced himself for a coming drought. Zander

wasn't an idiot. He knew it would be tougher to convince engaged couples to get married at the hotel since it was supposedly cursed, but he could tough it out for a few months. Once the Bennington actually managed to marry off a few couples, this whole debacle would blow over and everything would return to normal.

Of course that plan hinged on the fact that the weddings already on the books went as planned.

"You mean people believe in this curse so much that they want to move their weddings to a different location?" Unbelievable.

Ryan sighed. "So much so that they're willing to forgo the deposit. The Vows column carries some serious weight."

"We're not going to be able to dig our way out from under this until someone actually ties the knot here." Zander's head ached. What was he supposed to do? Drag people from the marriage-license line at city hall into his lobby with a priest and a wedding cake? "Tell me we've still got something coming up."

"I wish I could." Ryan crossed his arms. "As of right now, we don't have a single wedding scheduled in the ballroom until June."

Five months from now. He'd be bankrupt by then. "Unacceptable."

"It might be time to cut our rates."

Zander shook his throbbing head. "No."

The Bennington was one of the most luxurious hotels in the city. If word got around that they were lowering their rates, their lavish reputation would take a hit. It would also be a sure sign they were admitting defeat.

"There's only one desirable solution," Zander said.

Ryan's eyebrows lifted. "And that would be?"

"We get the Vows columnist to print a retraction." He'd tossed every possible solution around in his head, and it was the only surefire way to put an end to the curse rumors once and for all.

"That would be ideal. But how do we go about getting that done?"

"You chatted with the reporter. You two have a rapport. Why don't you wine and dine her a bit?" It was worth a shot.

Granted, Zander could wine and dine her himself. Page Six had named him one of the most eligible bachelors in Manhattan a year ago. He pretty much had the wining-and-dining routine down pat.

For some reason, he couldn't stomach the idea. He told himself it had nothing to do with Allegra's CEO-walk-of-shame comment. In fact, it would serve her right to see his picture in the society pages with his arm around another woman.

Since when do you care about making Allegra Clark jealous?

"You can't be serious," Ryan said flatly.

Zander cleared his throat. He needed to stop thinking about Allegra. She had nothing to do with this…

Except she sort of did. And not in a good way.

"You want me to date the reporter?" Ryan drew in a sharp breath, then released it. "Sorry, cousin, but that doesn't exactly fall under my job description as CFO."

"I didn't say you should date her. Just invite her to a nice dinner here at the hotel and politely ask her to reconsider the curse nonsense." Had the columnist ever actually been to the Bennington? Maybe a field trip was in order.

Ryan sighed. “I don’t know. Do you really think it will work?”

“I think it’s worth a shot.” Mainly because it was their only option at the moment.

“Fine. I’ll do it. Dinner, here at the hotel.” He leaned back in his chair and lifted an eyebrow. “But first you answer one question.”

Zander shrugged. “Shoot.”

“Why me?”

Zander’s gaze shifted to his empty espresso cup. “Who else would you suggest? The bellman?”

“You know that’s not what I meant. I want to know why you don’t want to take the reporter to dinner yourself.” He gave Zander a wry grin. “You’re deflecting.”

“I’m not deflecting.” He was *absolutely* deflecting.

And Ryan saw right through it. “This is about the Warren bride, isn’t it?”

Zander’s jaw tensed. “It’s most definitely not.”

After a brief pause, he added, “And don’t call her that. Her name’s Allegra. Allegra Clark.”

“I know. That was a test, and you failed.” Ryan snickered. “Big-time.”

“Don’t you have a phone call to make to the *Times*?” Zander picked up his Montblanc fountain pen, twirled it between his fingers and then set it back down again. He didn’t seem to know what to do with his hands all of a sudden.

“What’s the story there? You two were engaged a long time ago, right?”

“No, we weren’t.” Not exactly, especially since Allegra couldn’t even remember their conversation.

Ryan frowned. “This wasn’t the one who left you at the altar?”

Zander picked up the pen again and squeezed it. Hard. "That was Laura, and she didn't leave me at the altar. We agreed that getting married would have been a mistake. It was a mutual decision."

Would Zander have preferred that fateful conversation hadn't taken place in the church lobby just minutes before the ceremony was supposed to have begun? Hell, yes. But it had. He couldn't change history.

They'd hadn't been in love. Not really. And Laura had been right to wonder if Zander had been holding back. He had.

"If memory serves, Laura fled the church in her wedding gown." Ryan shook his head. "No wonder these runaway brides have you rattled."

"I'm not rattled." Zander tossed the pen onto his desk. It bounced a few times before clattering to a stop. Ryan shot him a meaningful glance. "My concern is for the hotel. Period."

"Yet you want me to 'wine and dine' the reporter instead of taking her to dinner yourself. And this decision has nothing whatsoever to do with the fact that Allegra Clark is staying at your brownstone?" Ryan lifted an accusatory eyebrow.

Zander hadn't shared that information, but naturally Ryan would have heard about it. Secrets weren't exactly a thing in the Wilde family.

"Forget it. I'll take the reporter to dinner myself." Zander shrugged.

"You sure about that?"

No. "I'm inviting her to dinner, not proposing marriage." Been there, done that, got the T-shirt. Never again. "I'll handle it. You're off the hook, cousin."

Ryan stood. "If you say so. You're the boss."

Yes, he was.

The boss. The one calling the shots. The one in charge.

Why did it feel so much the opposite?

Allegra enjoyed teaching the adult ballet class so much that she ended up taking on the toddler creative-movement class right afterward, followed by preballet for five- and six-year-olds. By that time, she was ready for a break, so she ran out to get soup and a loaf of crusty French bread for her and Emily.

The deli around the corner looked exactly the same as it had back in high school, when she and Zander had spent hours studying after dance class. Even their corner booth looked the same, down to the small tear in the red vinyl seat. A lump formed in Allegra's throat when she spotted it, for reasons she didn't care to contemplate. So she faced the other direction as she waited for her to-go order and passed the time by calling Spencer's assistant.

She couldn't put it off any longer. She needed her things. At the very least, she needed her purse and her phone. Max, the deli owner, recognized Allegra and very kindly let her borrow the deli's landline. She dialed the number before she lost her nerve.

"Allegra, are you okay? No one's heard from you since, well..." The secretary cleared her throat.

Since I ran out on my wedding and left your boss standing at the altar?

"I'm fine. I'm staying with an old childhood friend here in Manhattan." She injected as much cheer into her voice as she could manage. *See how fine I sound?* "I left some things at the hotel, though, and I'm wondering if you could send them to me."

She braced herself for an icy response or, worse, a flat-out *no.*

"Of course. I have them right here. I was hoping you'd call before we checked out."

Her kindness hurt far more than a cold shoulder would have because it meant only one thing—she knew why Allegra had run.

"Thank you." Allegra rattled off the Wilde School of Dance's address as quickly as she could and slammed the phone down as her first tear fell.

Did everyone *know?*

"Here you go." Max handed Allegra a brown paper bag. "It's great to see you again. Are you back in New York for good?"

"Just visiting."

Right. As if this trip down memory lane was nothing but a fabulous vacation instead of what it really was.

What was it exactly?

"Where's your young man? Is he here, too?"

Allegra blinked. He was obviously talking about Zander, and she had no clue how to answer the question.

"Never mind me. I'm just a nosy old man." He waved a hand. "Come see us again while you're here if you get a chance."

"I will." Allegra swallowed around the lump in her throat.

She couldn't get out of the deli fast enough. She felt transparent, as if Max could see right through her. As if he knew that the last time she'd sat in his corner booth, she'd been whole and now she wasn't. Hadn't been for almost as long as she could remember.

She blinked against the snow flurries swirling

through the air as she made her way back to the studio. Tears pricked her eyes, and she wasn't altogether sure whether they were a product of the icy wind or the stinging humiliation of the conversation with Spencer's assistant.

Did everyone know?

The question ran through her mind like a song on constant repeat. She wasn't even sure why.

What difference did it make? Did it really matter if Spencer's secretary knew he'd been cheating on her all along? Or if his entire staff knew?

Those people weren't her friends. The bigger question—the one that really mattered—was far more troubling.

Had Allegra herself known?

The truth had slapped her in the face just minutes before she walked down the aisle. It was kind of hard to ignore the sight of her fiancé sticking his tongue down her wedding planner's throat. Even a smooth-talking politician couldn't spin his way out of that awkward encounter.

He'd tried, of course. And then he'd begged. He just needed her to go through with the wedding, and they'd figure out the pesky infidelity issue later. The election was in less than three months. He needed the positive press. The blushing bride. The happy-ever-after.

Even if none of it was real.

She'd nearly gone through with it. Then, halfway down the aisle, she couldn't catch her breath. She'd stopped dead in her tracks and stared down at the swath of ivory carpet scattered with pink rose petals, unable to move. Unable to think. She could feel her heartbeat in her throat, and she was certain she would die right there in her wedding gown, choking on dread.

She hadn't had a panic attack in years. Not since she'd joined the ballet. It had to mean something. When she'd dashed out of the ballroom at the Bennington, she'd been convinced it was a sign. Her subconscious had been telling her she couldn't go through with it. She couldn't marry a man who so obviously didn't love her.

But now, standing on the threshold of the Wilde School of Dance with her heartbeat once again clogging her throat, she realized she'd gotten it wrong. The thought of marrying Spencer wasn't what had nearly caused her to crumple to the ground in raw fear. It had been the realization that she'd suspected just what kind of man Spencer was all along.

She'd known.

She'd known, and it had never really mattered because she wasn't in love with him. Yet she'd been ready to marry him, anyway. Because so long as she was married to someone she didn't love with her whole heart, she'd never be broken again.

She'd lost everything the day her mother, father and little sister died on the way to her dance recital. Her world had bottomed out. She couldn't live through that kind of loss a second time. What better way to protect herself against that kind of grief than to go through life without really loving? Without really living?

Oh, my God.

The pieces were coming together now with shameful clarity. How long had she been lying to herself? Weeks. Months. Years.

The paper bag from the deli slipped through her

fingers and fell onto the snow-covered sidewalk with a splat. She tried to bend down and pick it up, but she couldn't. She was paralyzed again. Her breath came in terrifying gulps, but she still couldn't seem to get enough air. She clawed at her throat. Everything around her—the crawling traffic, the pedestrians pushing past her, the frost-covered streetlamps—began to blur around the edges.

I'm losing my mind.

She squeezed her eyes closed and tried to fight it. But it was no use. Fear was pressing down, suffocating her until she could no longer stand.

She sank to her hands and knees, barely conscious of the frigid pavement and the gritty rock salt digging into her palms. Soup was spilling out of the bag she'd dropped, leaking all over the sidewalk. She took another desperate inhale. The rich scent of tomato and basil caused bile to rise to the back of her throat.

I'm going to be sick.

It was all she could do not to curl into a fetal position right there in the middle of midtown Manhattan.

"Allegra?"

Somewhere beyond the fog in her head, she was vaguely aware of a person calling her name. A man.

"Allegra! My God, what's wrong?"

She forced her eyes open.

Zander.

He was there. How? When?

Allegra had never been so grateful to see a familiar face in all her life. She tried to say his name, but couldn't force it out.

He crouched down so they were on eye level, and

the worry in his gaze was too much to bear. Too real. Too familiar.

She grabbed onto the lapels of his suit jacket.

Help me.

"Listen to me, sweetheart. You're okay. You're having a panic attack, but everything is going to be fine." He gathered her into his arms and pulled her to her feet.

Her knees buckled and she leaned into him, burying her face against his shoulder.

"Can you hear me?" he murmured into her hair. "Nod if you can."

She nodded against his chest, barely conscious of the smooth silk of his tie against her cheek.

"I'm here. I'm here, and I've got you." His hands moved in soothing circles over her back. "Breathe, Allegra. Just breathe."

It seemed impossible, but with a little more coaxing, she managed a shuddering inhale.

"That's good," he whispered. "Again. Take another breath."

She did as he said.

Her heart was still beating so hard that her chest burned like she'd just run a marathon, but the fog in her head was beginning to clear.

"Come with me. Let's get you home."

Home.

Allegra's frantic heart skipped a beat. She knew better than to argue with him. Couldn't if she tried.

Tears were streaming down her face. She was sobbing, and she wasn't altogether sure whether it was a reaction to the panic still coursing through her or the smallest sliver of relief.

This was the Zander she remembered, the Zander

who'd once held her when everything fell apart. He was taking her home.

Such a place almost seemed possible.

Almost.

Chapter Six

Only eleven minutes passed between the time Zander called for the Bennington's driver and the arrival of a sleek black limousine with the hotel's logo on the door. Eleven minutes in which he aged at least five years while Allegra clung to him like a wounded puppy.

He knew straightaway she was having a panic attack. Before his CEO days, Zander had been on duty as the hotel's general manager when a guest in one of the ballrooms experienced a similar incident. It had been years ago, but he'd never forgotten the raw fear in the young man's eyes. Zander had never felt quite so helpless in the face of suffering before.

Now he was seeing that same kind of fear shining back at him from the depths of Allegra's gaze, and it shook him to the core.

He'd held her while they waited for the car and spoke

as calmly as he could manage, whispering the same kind of assurances he'd given her on the day of her family's accident. Assurances that had turned out to be lies.

Everything's going to be okay.

I'm here.

I'll always be here.

He felt like the world's biggest impostor.

"Where to, Mr. Wilde?" the chauffeur asked, meeting Zander's gaze in the rearview mirror as the privacy divider began to rise. "The hotel?"

"No." Zander's voice was sharper than he intended, but Allegra didn't seem to notice. He cleared his throat. *Stay calm.* "To the brownstone, please."

That hadn't been the plan.

On the contrary, he'd spent the majority of his day figuring out a way to get Allegra out of his house. Once the housekeeping staff had completed their daily tasks and he'd gone over the reservations schedule with a fine-tooth comb, he'd located an available room on the eleventh floor.

It helped that Spencer Warren and his staff had cleared out, but he hadn't intended on sharing that information with Allegra. He'd simply planned on showing up at the dance school and handing her a key.

His throat grew thick just thinking about it. He'd felt so magnanimous. So damn charitable, when in reality, offering her a free seven-night stay in his hotel would have been purely self-serving.

He'd just wanted her as far out of his sight as possible. At minimum, out of his house. And now that room key sat nestled in his shirt pocket, directly beneath Allegra's tearstained cheek.

"We'll be home in just a minute." He bowed his head

to whisper into her hair, inhaling the lush scent of soft peonies in full bloom.

He closed his eyes. She smelled the same. Felt the same, nestled in his arms.

The same, but also different. Different in ways that were even more beguiling. More tempting. Just...*more.*

What the hell was he thinking, bringing her back to the brownstone?

This is a bad idea.

The worst. He was keenly aware of that fact, now that she was pressed against him. It felt too natural. Too much like she belonged there, next to his heartbeat.

But there was no way he was leaving her alone. Not when she was like this. Over his dead body.

"Your mother." Allegra looked up, wide-eyed, but remained tucked under his arm. "She's expecting me back in the studio. I told her I'd teach the afternoon classes. She's got to be wondering where I am."

"She's fine. I told her I was taking you home." He'd texted Emily as soon as he'd called for the limo and then set his phone to Vibrate. It had been buzzing away in his suit pocket ever since. He'd eventually switched it off completely.

The text messages and calls would have to wait.

"Thank you." Allegra voice was a hoarse whisper, and she gave him a wobbly smile. At the same time, a tear slid down her cheek.

Zander brushed it away with the pad of his thumb and then inexplicably let his fingertips linger on the delicate curve of her jaw.

Stop touching her.

The worst of the panic attack was over. She could breathe now, but she still looked dazed, with a faraway look in her eyes that was far too troubled for Zander's taste. He couldn't let her go. Not yet. "How long has this been going on, sweetheart?"

Sweetheart. Again.

In the back of his head, alarm bells rang.

"Awhile." Allegra's smile faded, drawing Zander's attention to her mouth. Every muscle in his body tensed. "It started after I moved away, after..."

He nodded. *After the accident.* He wasn't about to make her say it.

"But then the panic attacks stopped. For years." Her gaze shifted to her lap. "Until the other night."

Interesting. "The night of the wedding?"

She nodded.

Somehow that confession explained everything and nothing, all at once.

Then a horrific thought occurred to Zander, one he hadn't dared entertain before. "Did he hurt you? Because if he put his hands on you, if that's why..."

She blinked. "What? No! It wasn't like that."

He looked at her.

What was it like, then?

The question hovered between them, unspoken. But very much there.

Allegra inhaled a ragged breath. "He was cheating on me. I found out only minutes before the ceremony."

Zander's hands clenched into fists, and it was only then that he realized he was still touching her. Still stroking her cheek. "That bastard."

She rolled her eyes, but Zander couldn't help noticing a hint of a smile on her lips. At last, he let himself relax.

She's fine.

"I know you're in hero mode right now, but you can turn down the testosterone a notch or two. It's more complicated than it sounds." There she was—the impertinent runaway bride who'd crashed his birthday party.

Zander had missed that spunk more than he'd realized. Still, he didn't want to push. Not after he'd just found her on her hands and knees on a Manhattan sidewalk, unable to breathe. "We don't have to talk about this now."

"Good." She closed her eyes and let her head fall back onto his arm.

Zander's fingertips drifted lower until he was touching her neck. He moved his thumb up and down in the same tender circles he'd been tracing on her cheek. If it had been anyone else, it would have felt strange. Maybe even wrong. But they'd been dance partners.

Back when they were teenagers, they'd practiced for so many hours a day that sometimes Zander wasn't sure where his body ended and Allegra's began. Now that the icy wall between them had begun to thaw, it was all too easy to slip back into old patterns.

Muscle memory. That's all it is.

Just one body remembering another—remembering the dip of her lower back beneath his palm, the perfect fit of her hand in his. Once upon a time, those things had been familiar. Natural.

Innocent.

As right as it might feel now, the innocence that had once come with touching Allegra was notably absent. That was the difference, at least on his end. They weren't kids anymore. They were all grown-up.

He took a measured breath and focused his attention on the snow beating against the car window and the pale glow of the streetlights against the deepening winter sky instead of the woman in his arms.

Within minutes, she fell asleep, burrowing even closer. Zander did his best to keep his thoughts trained on practical matters. Mundane details, like how he'd need to get back to the dance school at some point to pick up his car, which he'd left parked at the curb, and the pile of paperwork that was no doubt piling up on his desk. He couldn't quite focus, though, and before long, he found himself watching Allegra sleep. The little furrow between her eyebrows vanished. Her whole body seemed to sigh, and for the first time since he'd found her cowering on the sidewalk, she looked almost peaceful. Content.

When the car turned onto Riverside Drive and the Hudson River came into view through a snowy haze, he gave her a gentle shake. "We're almost home."

Her eyelids fluttered open. Their eyes held for a second too long, and the awareness that Zander had been fighting for the duration of the ride settled over him with undeniable clarity. For the first time in years, he and Allegra were alone together. The chauffeur sat beyond the privacy divider, feet away. It might as well have been a mile.

He swept a lock of hair from her face and felt the full force of her glittering blue gaze deep in his chest. "Feeling better?"

She nodded. "Thank you again. I'm a bit embarrassed now…"

"Don't be. It was nothing." He swallowed. Hard.

He was lying, and they both knew it. Finding her like that—taking care of her, making sure she was safe—was definitely *something*. It had been for him, anyway.

"I mean it. I'm glad you were there." She licked her lips, and once again, Zander's gaze was drawn to her mouth. His heart stuttered to a near stop. "I'm glad you're here now."

Then her lips parted ever so slightly, and she pressed a gentle kiss to the corner of his mouth. Their faces were so close together that she only had to lift her head a fraction of an inch, but Zander still saw it coming. He could have changed what was about to happen.

A better man would have.

But Zander didn't want to be a better man. Not at that moment.

He'd waited a lifetime to kiss Allegra Clark.

She was dreaming.

Allegra had forgotten how exhausted she always felt after a panic attack, like she wanted to sleep for days.

Sometimes she had, especially in the weeks and months after she'd first moved to Cambridge. During the first six months she lived with her aunt, she'd missed twenty-seven days of school. Most of those days had been spent in bed. The others had been spent developing coping techniques—relearning how to breathe, relearning how to *live*.

Once she'd started dancing again, life had gotten easier. Not ballroom dancing, obviously. The thought of dancing with anyone other than Zander was out of the question.

Ballet, on the other hand, was perfect. She loved its classical roots, dating all the way back to the nineteenth century. Ballet was steeped in tradition. It was predictable. It was demanding, to be sure, but it would never surprise her. Never leave her reeling. She knew exactly what to expect when she showed up for class every day—a half hour at the barre, followed by a combination at center, a graceful adagio, a brisk allegro and, at the end, a reverence.

The predictability of it was a balm. Ballet helped her heal. Or so she'd thought.

The panic attack she'd had this afternoon was one of the worst she'd ever experienced. No wonder she could barely keep her eyes open.

But the dream felt so vivid. So real.

Zander was there and his mouth was on hers, kissing her. Tasting her.

Actually, *she'd* been the one to kiss *him*. Just a tender press of her lips. But then she'd let out a little groan for some insane reason, and now her tongue was sliding against his. The kiss became something else entirely, something wholly decadent. And it felt so good, so perfect. Fated somehow. As if this is what she'd been waiting for all along.

That's how she knew it was a dream. Real kisses didn't feel like this. Certainly not kisses between friends, and that's precisely what Zander was. A friend. That's what he'd always been, even in the past day, when they hadn't been on the friendliest terms.

Although the relief that had coursed through her when he'd scooped her up from the sidewalk had been shockingly intense. And when he'd called her *sweetheart*, something had come loose inside her. Something she'd been trying very hard to keep bound up tight.

Those things had been real. Could the kiss be just

a dream? A thoroughly wonderful, thoroughly *confusing* dream.

"Mr. Wilde, we've arrived."

The voice came from somewhere overhead and startled her into consciousness. She dragged her eyes open. Everything seemed to be moving in slow motion. Her body felt warm all over. Liquid and sweet, like melted honey.

But when Zander's face came into focus just inches from hers, she froze.

This was no dream.

What have I done?

They looked at one another for a long, loaded moment. He seemed just as stunned by the sudden turn of events as she felt. Maybe even more so, if the small shake of his head was any indication.

"I shouldn't have let that happen." His gaze darted to her mouth and then just as quickly flew back to meet hers. "You're upset, and I..."

Allegra swallowed. Nodded. Although she wasn't quite sure what she was agreeing with.

What? I'm upset, and you're what *exactly?* She wanted to interrogate him before they got out of the car and pretended none of this ever happened.

Because that was definitely Zander's intention. His jaw was clenched tight, and his eyes—dark and wild only seconds before—were now steely with determination.

"Mr. Wilde," the driver prompted.

Zander reached across Allegra to press a button on the car's ceiling. "Yes, Tony. Miss Clark and I are ready."

Allegra shook her head. She wasn't ready. If she

tried to stand right now, her legs probably wouldn't be capable of holding her up.

What was wrong with her? She didn't feel panicked anymore. Quite the opposite, actually.

She should definitely be capable of standing.

The phrase *weak in the knees* popped into her mind. She shook her head again.

No.

Just...

No.

She couldn't be attracted to Zander Wilde. She was working at his mother's dance studio. She was living *in his house*. The night before, she'd nearly married another man.

But Zander thought that big white wedding gown had been for him. Remember?

She blinked. Hard.

Zander had slid to the other end of the car, leaving an enormous expanse of smooth leather seat between them. As if that wasn't symbolic enough, he refused to make eye contact with her. He straightened the Windsor knot in his tie, cleared his throat and then straightened it again.

"Zander, I..."

The door closest to Allegra flew open. Beyond a swirl of snow, she could see a man in an overcoat and hat offering her his hand. Tony, presumably.

Somewhere in the periphery, Allegra caught a glimpse of a dash of black fur. It was the kitten she'd seen earlier from the window.

"Go on," Zander prompted.

She turned to face him again. "But..."

But what? She took a deep breath.

But I just kissed you.

"Don't worry. You won't be alone. I'll be inside in a few minutes. I need to make a call first." Zander pulled an iPhone from his pocket. He pressed the home button, but the screen remained dark. The phone wasn't even turned on.

"You should go on up and get some rest. I'm sure you're exhausted." He slipped the phone back out of sight. When he glanced at her again, he was wearing his CEO expression. Impassive and businesslike, to the point of looking utterly disinterested.

But his eyes betrayed him. Those familiar green irises of his were anything but neutral.

"Right." She nodded, and her face grew warm.

Zander was being a gentleman. He was offering her an out, a chance to pretend the kiss never happened.

He knew she'd been vulnerable. She'd been so disoriented that she'd almost believed the kiss had been a dream.

Hadn't she?

Of course. She never would have kissed him otherwise.

Maybe.

Probably.

But as she placed her hand in Tony's to climb out of the car and leave Zander behind, she didn't feel quite so confused anymore. The fog in her head had lifted. Her heartbeat was steady and strong. For the most part, she felt back to normal again. Like herself.

Yet somehow, undeniably, disappointed.

Chapter Seven

Zander should have known something disastrous had happened the minute he walked through the Bennington's revolving door the following morning. To an outsider, everything probably seemed perfectly in order. Fresh flowers topped every available surface, the gold clock hanging from the lobby ceiling chimed right on time and the chandeliers shone in perfection.

But Zander was no outsider.

He knew the Bennington inside and out. He knew the bellmen were darting about not because they were busier than usual, but because they were studiously avoiding his gaze. He knew the manager's smile seemed just a bit strained around the edges. And he definitely knew that the selection of newspapers next to the coffee service seemed smaller than usual.

Something was missing.

Namely the *New York Times*.

He stopped at the coffee station long enough to pour himself a double espresso and then bypassed his darkened office to head straight for Ryan's.

"Good morning." He stood in Ryan's open doorway and sipped his coffee, hoping he was wrong. Maybe everything was perfectly in order. Maybe he was just imagining things. Maybe the *Times* delivery was simply running late. It wasn't unheard-of.

He didn't want to deal with another crisis this morning. Not after the day he'd had yesterday. Not after the kiss that he and Allegra were still pretending never happened.

Ryan looked up from his computer monitor and narrowed his gaze. "You're alive."

"The last time I checked, yes. Alive and well." Zander unbuttoned his suit jacket and took a seat.

Alive and well.

The last part was debatable, despite the fact that the day before had been his first afternoon off in as long as he could remember.

He'd kept his word to Allegra and stayed at the brownstone while she'd slept. He would have been useless at the office, anyway. Her panic attack had left him shaken.

The kiss that followed had just about killed him.

Ryan leaned forward and pinned Zander with a glare. "You left yesterday to run a mysterious errand and never returned. What the hell happened to you?"

A lot had happened. Too much. But he wasn't about to get into it with his cousin.

"Something came up," he said tersely.

"That's it? Something came up?" Ryan snorted. "I

hope it was important, because the *Times* skewered us this morning."

What now? Zander shook his head. "That doesn't make sense. The Vows column only runs on weekends. Don't tell me the actual News section has developed an interest in our alleged curse."

Impossible.

A trickle of dread snaked its way down Zander's spine. Ryan knew better than to joke about something this serious.

"The front page couldn't care less, but the New York City section sure has something to say about it." Ryan swiveled in his chair, grabbed a newspaper off his credenza and threw it down on the desk.

Zander scanned the page. If the hotel was getting more bad press, he'd have to take action. It couldn't go on. He wondered who was responsible, who he'd need to fire.

Then at last his gaze landed on a headline in the lower left-hand corner, revealing the identity of the offender.

Zander himself.

Bennington CEO a No-Show for Dinner Meeting, Leaving All of Manhattan Wondering: Is the Bridal Curse Real?

Zander clenched his gut. He'd completely forgotten about dinner with the reporter. No wonder Ryan had thought he'd been dead in a ditch somewhere.

Damn it.

Ryan cleared his throat. His hands were folded neatly in front of him on the surface of his desk. He seemed perfectly unruffled, rather like the polished veneer of the hotel lobby. He didn't have to spell things out for Zander, though.

They were well and truly screwed.

"Am I missing something here? I thought we agreed that you'd handle the reporter," Ryan said.

"We did." Zander nodded and somehow managed to tear his gaze away from the lurid headline.

"Then why didn't you show up?" A telltale angry vein throbbed to life in Ryan's temple.

As CEO, Zander was technically Ryan's boss. But CFO was pretty high up on the food chain. They'd always operated as more of a team, and Zander preferred it that way. Plus, they were both Wildes. They were family. Zander trusted Ryan with his life and vice versa.

But now, for the first time in his professional life, Zander had dropped the ball. Big-time.

He swallowed. "I forgot."

"You *forgot*?"

Zander nodded again. It was a piss-poor excuse, but it was the truth. "Why didn't any of the staff call me when she got here? I could have headed straight over. Being late would've been bad but infinitely preferable to standing her up."

He was grasping at straws, and they both knew it. The dinner had been Zander's responsibility. No one else's.

How could he have let this happen?

He closed his eyes. A headache was already blossoming at the base of his skull, no doubt because he knew precisely why he'd forgotten his date with the Vows reporter.

Allegra.

"The staff did call you. Multiple times. Then they called me, and I rang you for hours. When you never answered, I came here myself, but she'd already given up and gone home."

Where she'd obviously spent her evening writing another story about the supposed curse rather than being wined and dined. The City section had apparently been happy to put it in print for the world to see.

Perfect. Just perfect.

Zander reached into the pocket of his suit jacket for his phone. Sure enough, the screen was dark. He'd never turned it back on after he'd found Allegra kneeling on the sidewalk in a puddle of soup.

He turned on the phone and immediately got dinged with dozens of texts and voice mail notifications.

Too little, too late.

"Do you want to tell me what's going on? It's not like you to be this distracted. Although I have a feeling I already know the answer." Ryan lifted an eyebrow. "It's the runaway bride, isn't it?"

Zander stared at him and said nothing.

"Don't bother asking which bride I'm talking about, because we both know who I mean."

Zander clenched his jaw. "She has a name."

He couldn't stomach thinking of Allegra as *the runaway bride*. Not after hearing why she'd run. And definitely not after she'd kissed him.

"I'm going to take that comment as a *yes*," Ryan said.

Zander sighed. "Fine. I was with Allegra yesterday, but it's not what you think."

Not entirely, anyway.

"I rearranged some reservations yesterday and found her a room here. I thought it would be better for everyone involved if she stayed here instead of at the brownstone. She's teaching at my mother's dance school, so I went down there to give her a key." Zander paused.

He took a sip of his espresso and wished it was something stronger, possibly a manhattan. Then again, he'd already mucked things up enough. Now wasn't the time to start drinking during the day.

"And?" Ryan crossed his arms.

"And it wasn't the right time," Zander said quietly.

Ryan deserved an explanation. But as much as Zander owed him one, telling him about Allegra's panic attack seemed wrong.

He leveled his gaze at his cousin. "I realize that sounds vague, but you're just going to have to trust me. Can you do that?"

After a loaded silence, Ryan nodded. "Of course I can. I wouldn't be here if it wasn't for you."

"Thank you."

He didn't deserve such blind trust. Not after the massive mistake he'd just made. But he was grateful for it, all the same.

"We've got some major damage control to contend with, though." Ryan scrubbed a hand over his face. "I can't imagine how you're going to get in the Vows columnist's good graces now. Celestia Lane has you in her crosshairs."

"I think a direct approach is the best option." Zander scrolled through the contacts in his phone until he reached the listing for the *Times* switchboard.

Ryan's eyebrows lifted all the way to his hairline. "You think a phone call is going to take care of this?"

"It's worth a try." Zander shrugged, pressed Call and asked the receptionist to connect him to the Vows desk. Hold music blared in his ear while he did his best to ignore the smirk on his cousin's face.

"She's not going to take your call. You know that, right?"

Zander shrugged. "Sure she will. She's a journalist. Doesn't she have to take my call?"

"I'm beginning to believe you don't know anything about journalism." Ryan's smirk became larger and exponentially more annoying. "Or women, for that matter."

Zander arched an eyebrow. "I know plenty about women."

"I'm not talking about sex. I'm talking about *women.* Their emotions. What makes them tick, that sort of thing. Surely you know you have a tendency to come off a little cold?"

Zander's response was a disbelieving stare. His own cousin thought that highly of him?

He wasn't cold. And he knew more about women than simply how to get them into bed.

He knew that daisies had always been Allegra's favorite flower, which is why he'd been taken aback when they'd been notably absent from her bridal bouquet. He knew that *Jane Eyre* had been her favorite book since the day before her fourteenth birthday, when she'd read it from cover to cover in a single, uninterrupted sitting. And now, after yesterday, he also knew all about the delicious little sighing noise she made when she was being kissed.

So soft. So perfectly sweet. Like a kitten.

Perhaps those details only proved Ryan's point. Zander might not know everything about women, but he knew enough about one of them.

Allegra.

The only one who mattered.

Used to matter, he corrected himself.

They might have had a *moment* yesterday in the limo, but nothing about his relationship with Allegra had changed. After fourteen long years of silence, they were still virtual strangers. The kiss hadn't meant anything. She'd been disoriented. Disoriented and, most of all, grateful.

He'd taken care of her. Anyone else in his position would have done the same thing. It didn't make him a hero. It certainly didn't make him a love interest. It made him a friend.

Except friends didn't typically kiss one another the way Allegra had kissed him.

The receptionist returned to the line. "I'm sorry, Mr. Wilde, but Ms. Lane can't take your call at this time."

Zander cleared his throat. "I see."

The receptionist hung up on him before he could thank her.

Ryan leaned back in his chair. "I think now is when I get to say I told you so."

Zander chose to ignore that little barb. "It's not a problem. If the reporter won't take my calls, I'll just have to come up with another plan."

"Let me know when you get that figured out," Ryan said.

"Will do." Zander stood and made his way to the door. Call him crazy, but he preferred discussing business without being psychoanalyzed.

Particularly when it came to Allegra.

Afraid of what you'll find out?

Maybe.

Then again, maybe not. He was already painfully aware that the longer she'd been back, the more of a mess his life had become. He'd known he was in trouble the minute she crashed his birthday party.

He just hadn't realized quite how much until she'd kissed him.

It took the better part of the morning for Allegra to convince Emily that she was indeed well enough to make the trip to the dance school again and teach class. They hadn't left the house yet, so she still wasn't entirely sure she'd been successful.

She wanted to teach. She *needed* it. If she stayed at the brownstone all day, she'd have nothing to do but think about the events of the day before.

She'd kissed him.

Zander.

As if her life wasn't already so complicated that she'd ended up on a Manhattan sidewalk practically in the fetal position, she'd gone and kissed her best friend.

Correction: *former* best friend.

Although he'd certainly acted like a best friend the day before. More than a best friend, if she was being honest.

She might have been the one to initiate the kiss, but he'd certainly been an eager participant. Eager and *capable.*

Where on earth had he learned to kiss like that, anyway?

Stop obsessing.

"It was just a kiss. I'm probably making a huge deal

out of nothing, right?" Allegra set a warm bowl of milk down on the front steps of the brownstone in front of the tiny black kitten that she'd once again spotted tip-toeing through the snow.

The kitten let out a loud mew, which sounded too much like an argumentative commentary for Allegra's liking.

"Fine. I know I said it was the best kiss I'd ever had, but I was hardly in a condition to properly evaluate it. I was semiconscious at best."

That was a stretch, but what the kitten didn't know wouldn't hurt her.

Allegra wrapped her coat more tightly around her shivering frame while she watched the little cat lap up the milk. At least she'd gotten a few of her things back. Finally.

After she'd climbed out of Zander's limo, made her way upstairs and fallen into bed, she'd slept straight through until morning. When she'd finally gotten up, she'd found her handbag, cell phone and pale pink cashmere coat lined up neatly on the downstairs sofa. The overnight bag she'd brought to the Bennington from Cambridge had been sitting right beside them. At long last, she was wearing her own clothes.

Her cell phone had needed charging, which was no big surprise. She'd plugged it in, wondering if Zander had laid everything out so neatly for her or whether it had been Emily. Then she wondered why on earth she cared. Zander wasn't even home. He'd left for work before she'd gotten out of bed, even though it had been early. She wasn't altogether sure what that meant either, although she suspected he was avoiding her.

It didn't matter. She had everything she needed for the time being. Clothes, the little bit of money in her purse, even a job. A temporary job, anyway. Just not a home.

"I guess we have that in common, don't we?" she muttered.

The kitten mewed and wound her way around Allegra's legs until the front door of the brownstone opened and the tiny cat dashed away.

"Did I hear you talking to someone out here?" Emily scanned the empty porch with her gaze.

Oh, you know, I was just talking to a stray kitten about kissing your son yesterday. Totally normal conversation.

"No." Allegra straightened, trying her best to look sane. "I mean, yes. But it was just a cat—the little black one I keep seeing out here."

Emily frowned. "In this weather? The poor thing could freeze."

"I brought her some warm milk and she seemed to enjoy it, but she bolted when the door opened just now."

Allegra squinted toward the horizon, but she couldn't spot the kitten. The animal had disappeared somewhere beyond the slow-moving taxicabs and the steam rising from the slick black streets.

Allegra turned back toward Emily. "You haven't seen her out here? Ever?"

"No, not at all." Emily shook her head and slid her key into the lock on the front door.

"That's so odd. She seems to be out here every time I look out the window." If it hadn't been for the empty saucer at Allegra's feet, she might have wondered if she'd been seeing things. Which would have been the icing on the cake of the tumultuous past week.

She swallowed and headed down the front steps of the brownstone. Today would be different. It had to be.

It wasn't until she reached the sidewalk that she realized Emily was still standing on the welcome mat, eyeing her with concern. "Are you sure you feel up to coming to the studio today? I can handle things if you need more rest."

"I'm fine." She pasted a smile on her face. "Honestly, Emily, I need to keep busy. I enjoyed teaching yesterday even more than I expected. I'd like to work at the studio for a while. Would that be all right?"

A while. Allegra wasn't even sure what that meant. Days? Weeks?

Fortunately, Emily didn't ask her to elaborate. "It's more than all right. It's perfect. The kids loved you yesterday."

"Good." Allegra nodded.

The day progressed with much less drama than the previous one. Emily insisted on running out to pick up lunch, which was perfectly understandable since Allegra had never returned from her ill-fated soup run.

She was alone in the studio for the first time. Just her and the memories.

Memories of learning how to waltz in Zander's arms. Memories of the way he'd held her—like she was something to be treasured. Revered.

If she was being honest with herself, yesterday hadn't been the first time she'd thought about kissing him. She'd thought about it once or twice when they were teenagers. More often than that, actually.

But he was *Zander*. Her dance partner. Her best friend. He probably would have laughed in her face if she'd just kissed him out of nowhere.

Allegra's fingertips grazed her lips as she let herself dwell on the memory of their kiss in the back of the limousine. The heat of it. The taste of it, rich with years of unspoken yearning.

Maybe he wouldn't have laughed if she'd kissed him all those years ago after all.

He certainly hadn't laughed yesterday. He'd kissed her right back, like a dying man in need of oxygen. Then he'd pushed her out of the car and steadfastly ignored her ever since.

She wouldn't make that mistake again. Not even while semiconscious.

Starting immediately, she also wouldn't keep dwelling on it. Being alone in the studio was sort of nice, if she ignored the weight of yesterday hanging in the air. It gave her a chance to slip into pointe shoes and try a few advanced ballet combinations.

She flipped through Emily's collection of record albums until she found music that was familiar from her tenure at the Boston Ballet. *Giselle.*

Allegra placed the needle of the record player down in the middle of the album, right at the start of the second act.

As a member of the corps de ballet, Allegra had never been a prima ballerina. She wasn't a star or even a soloist. Corps dancers performed together as a group. Their role in a ballet company was to move together as one. To blend in. In most productions, they served as little more than a beautiful backdrop to the principal dancers.

Giselle was different. Its second act was known as a *ballet blanc*. A white ballet. The corps dancers all wore sweeping white tulle. They were the real stars of *Giselle*'s Act II, portraying the spirits of doomed, heartbroken brides. They moved as one, hauntingly beautiful in their long, romantic tutus and gossamer wedding veils.

The irony wasn't lost on Allegra. It seemed oddly prophetic that *Giselle* had been one of the last ballets she'd performed. But like most dancers in the corps, she adored it. Dancing *Giselle* had been the highlight of her career. The moment the studio was filled with Adolphe Adam's familiar score, the steps came back to her as naturally as if she'd danced them just days ago, rather than two long years.

She closed her eyes and slid into a *glissade*. Once, twice. Three times. The next step was an excruciatingly slow, controlled *développé*. Allegra pointed her right foot and smoothly, slowly, slid it along her left calf. When it reached her knee, she unfolded her leg until was fully extended, stretched high above her head.

She held it there, relishing the tender ache in her muscles. It felt good to move like this again. Right, somehow. Dancing had always made her feel strong. Whole. Invincible, even in her darkest days.

She opened her eyes, seeking her reflection in the classroom's mirrored walls. But the first thing her gaze landed on wasn't her own image. It was Zander's.

He was standing at the back at the room with his arms crossed, leaning languidly against the wall. Quietly watching her dance.

Allegra met his gaze in the mirror. She went breathless for a few beats until looking at him became too much and she stumbled out of her *développé*.

What is he *doing here?*

What reason could a hotel CEO possibly have for repeatedly dropping by his mother's dance school?

Allegra swept an errant strand of hair back into her ballerina bun as she marched toward the record player, the toe boxes of her pointe shoes tip-tapping on the hard floor. When she plucked the needle from the album, the silence that descended over the room felt stifling. Swollen with something she couldn't quite name.

"Zander." She cleared her throat and turned to face him.

"Allegra." He pushed off the wall and came closer, hands clenching briefly in his pockets.

His gaze traveled slowly down her body and finally landed on the pink ribbons crisscrossing her ankles. She felt like hiding for some silly reason.

He looked up again, and there was an unmistakable reverence in his dark eyes. "I assumed you were helping with the ballroom classes. You didn't tell me you were a ballerina now."

You didn't ask. "Used to be. I'm not a ballerina anymore."

"Not from where I'm standing. That was lovely." His voice went quiet. Rough. Allegra could feel its deep timbre in the pit of her belly. Then he cleared his throat and sounded like himself again. "I didn't expect to see you here. Emily swore up and down she'd make you stay home today."

Allegra hated the tug of disappointment she felt at the realization that he hadn't come to the dance school looking for her. For a minute she'd allowed herself to think that he wasn't actually avoiding her, but indeed he was.

Her face burned with embarrassment, followed very

quickly by irritation. She *worked* at the studio. She wasn't going to apologize for being there. "Do you always call your mother by her first name?"

He frowned. "Not always. Here, I do. Sometimes. Why do you ask?"

Allegra crossed her arms and steadfastly refused to look at his lips. "I don't know. It just seems a little..."

"Cold?" His left eyebrow arched.

"I was going to say strange." She cleared her throat.

Over Zander's shoulder, she could see their recital picture hanging on the lobby wall. She wanted to ask him why he'd stopped dancing after she left, but she was afraid of the answer.

"Your mom, I mean *Emily*, should be back any minute. I'm assuming you stopped by to see her?"

"I did, but I can't stay." Zander reached into the inside pocket of his suit jacket and pulled out an envelope. "Would you give this to her?"

"Sure, but like I said, she should be back soon." Allegra's fingertips brushed against his as she took the envelope. For a prolonged second, they both froze—hands touching, neither saying a word.

Zander's gaze dropped to her mouth, then he quickly looked away. Stepped back.

He shook his head. "I have to get back to the hotel."

"Right now?" God, she was pathetic. The way her voice cracked, it sounded like she was begging him to stay.

She didn't even *want* him to stay.

Did she?

"Yes." He gave her a tight smile. "It's cursed, remember?"

"Right." She nodded. "I'll see you later."

"Not tonight, I'm afraid. I'll be out late."

"Sometime, then." She turned to face the record player, because this weird goodbye was getting much too awkward all of a sudden.

Just go away. Please go.

He did.

She watched him walk away in the floor-to-ceiling mirror. Then she turned the music back on, and even though she knew it was just her mind playing tricks on her, she thought she caught a glimpse of herself in her costume from *Giselle*. The diaphanous tulle skirt, the long white veil.

So beautifully doomed.

Forever a bride.

Forever alone.

Chapter Eight

Allegra was mildly curious about the contents of the envelope Zander left in her care.

Scratch that. She was aggressively curious. Curious to the point of almost giving in to her urge to hold it up to the light after he'd gone.

The Bennington Hotel's crest was embossed on the upper right-hand corner, but otherwise it was blank. Allegra couldn't see a thing through the thick cream-colored paper. The Bennington apparently didn't skimp in the stationery department.

This was for the best, obviously. Whatever was inside that envelope was none of her business. The odds of the contents having anything to do with her were slim to none.

She wasn't even sure *why* she was so curious, other than it might provide some insight into the mysterious

Zander Wilde, teen-ballroom-dancer-turned-buttoned-up-CEO and expert kisser. Which, again, was none of her business whatsoever.

What on earth was wrong with her? She'd never spied on anyone before. Not once. She'd never been one of those girlfriends who went through her partner's phone or scrolled through email messages. Maybe if she had, she wouldn't have been quite so surprised by Spencer's extracurricular activities.

Then again, maybe she just hadn't cared enough to pull a Nancy Drew where her ex-fiancé was concerned.

She swallowed. That wasn't exactly something to be proud of. Neither was poking her nose where it so clearly didn't belong. She placed the envelope on the chair in Emily's office, where she'd be sure to see it, and busied herself with selecting music for the afternoon classes.

But as it turned out, the contents of the envelope did indeed have something to do with her. Sort of.

At the end of the day, Emily presented Allegra with her first paycheck. She tried to give it back. After all, she'd only completed a day and a half of work, and she was also living in Emily's house.

But Emily had been adamant, and frankly, Allegra needed the money if she was ever going to move out of the brownstone.

And she was *definitely* moving out. She just had a few things to care of first. Like finding an affordable apartment. Emphasis on *affordable*.

So you're actually moving back to New York? Permanently?

She wasn't sure she was ready to think about that quite yet, which was probably the only benefit of not being in a position to rent her own place.

"Thank you." Allegra glanced down at the check in her hand, noticing right away that something was wrong.

For starters, it was made out for far too much money. She'd have to teach a month's worth of classes to earn that much. Possibly more. Then her eyes focused on the signature at the bottom of the check, and she saw Zander's name.

"Emily, I think there's been a mistake." She stared at the amount again. So many zeros.

Then her gaze flitted to the name of the payee. Sure enough, the check wasn't for her. It was made out to a real estate management company.

"What, dear?" Emily said absently.

"This is the wrong check." Allegra handed it to Emily as it dawned on her that she was holding the contents of Zander's mysterious envelope.

This had to be it. His signature was right there at the bottom of the check, and his name was printed in its upper left-hand corner.

Emily squinted at the rectangular slip of paper, then reached for her reading glasses. "Oh, goodness, you're right. I've been swamped all day setting up the online registration forms for next semester's classes. This is what I get for trying to do too many things at once."

She opened a folder on her desk and exchanged the check for another one inside. "Here you go."

"Thank you." Allegra glanced at the check. This one had her name written on it, along with a much more modest dollar amount.

"I'm sorry I can't pay you more. Things have been a little tight around here recently. It seems there's a dance school popping up on every street corner these days. I'm finding it hard to compete."

"Don't apologize. Please." Emily had already been kinder than Allegra had any right to expect. "I hate to hear that the school is struggling, though. Is there anything I can do to help?"

"Your just being here is helpful. We can certainly use your ballet expertise since Tessa doesn't have time to teach much anymore. I'm thrilled for her, of course. But the students and parents like to know their ballet teacher has professional experience. In a way, you're a godsend right now." Emily squeezed her hand. "Not just because you're family."

Allegra's lips curved into a stiff smile.

She wasn't family.

She hadn't been part of a family in a very long time.

Allegra folded the check into a tiny square to stop her hands from trembling. Before she realized what she was doing, she'd practically transformed it into an origami swan.

She unzipped her dance bag and shoved it inside. "I hope you don't mind my asking, but that other check looked like it might have been for the school's rent."

Emily sighed. "It is. Can you believe how much they're charging for this building these days?"

Allegra nodded, but she wasn't thinking about the dollar amount, although it was indeed astronomical. She was thinking about the masculine signature scrawled across the bottom. "*Zander* pays for this building?"

"He does." Emily's mouth tipped into a half grin. "I'm guessing he never filled you in on the situation at the brownstone."

Allegra shook her head. Had she actually asked that question out loud?

Where was her filter? Gone. Along with the rest of her self-control, apparently.

"Never mind. I'm sorry I said anything." Allegra's face suddenly felt impossibly hot. "It's none of my business."

But her subconscious was screaming.

What situation at the brownstone?

"He owns it now," Emily said.

Allegra went very still. Zander owned the Wilde family brownstone?

No. That wasn't possible. The house had been in the family for years, passed down from one generation to the next. Someday it would belong to Zander, along with Tessa and Chloe. But not now. Not yet.

Unless…

Emily nodded. "He bought it from me three years ago. I was going to close the school. The thought of it broke my heart, but financially, I couldn't keep it going anymore."

Allegra swallowed. She couldn't imagine the West Village without the Wilde School of Dance. It had become part of the landscape, as vital to the neighborhood as Magnolia Bakery and Pier 45.

"Zander wanted to help. I couldn't let him do it long-term. I just couldn't. So I offered him the brownstone instead. The generous down payment infused the school with a nice sum of cash, and he's paying out the rest by taking over the school's rent." Emily's smile was so sad that Allegra couldn't quite look the older woman in the eye any longer.

She sank into the chair on the opposite side of the desk and dropped her gaze to her lap. What Emily was saying didn't bode well for the future of the Wilde School of Dance. It also meant something even more unsettling.

Zander was her landlord. And possibly, sort of, her boss, too.

This changed things. Allegra wasn't altogether sure why or how, but it did.

"This place means a lot to him." Emily turned her gaze toward the classroom, with its shiny, mirrored walls and old wood floor, nicked with memories. "Probably more than you know."

Allegra returned to the brownstone at the end of the day with tender feet and a full heart. It had been months since she'd spent all day in ballet shoes. She hadn't realized how much she'd missed it.

Teaching wasn't at all like being part of a professional dance company, obviously. In many ways, it was better. All joy, no pressure. She could see herself getting used to it.

Don't get ahead of yourself.

She had no business contemplating staying on at the Wilde School of Dance, no matter how often her thoughts kept spinning in that direction, so the sight of the little black kitten tiptoeing along the kitchen window ledge was a welcome distraction.

Allegra paused in the middle of the room and let her dance bag fall to her feet. The kitten peered at her through the glass. The animal's ears were pricked forward, and one of them had a tiny nick near the tip.

"Hi there." Allegra took a tentative step toward the window.

The kitten stayed put. As Allegra drew closer, she

noticed the cat's slight frame was shivering. A thin layer of snow coated her ebony fur.

Allegra bit her lip. "Maybe I can bring you inside. Only for a minute."

Emily had gone straight to her book club after the school closed. But her earlier comments led Allegra to believe she wouldn't be opposed to letting the kitten into the house.

This isn't her house anymore, remember?

Allegra swallowed. She definitely remembered.

The kitten pranced back and forth the length of the ledge, pawing at the window.

Allegra sighed. "Fine. I'll let you in just long enough to get you warm and dry. But it's got to be our little secret, okay?"

She unlatched the window, and the cat leaped into her arms.

"You're trembling." She kissed the kitten's dainty little head and held her close. Her soft coat smelled like winter—frosty leaves with a hint of roasted chestnuts.

Allegra wrapped the kitten in the blanket slung over the back of the living-room sofa and checked her newly charged phone. According to the device's display screen, her voice mail was full. Not a surprise, considering she'd recently been the subject of a column in the *New York Times*.

Sure enough, the messages all seemed to have something to do with her canceled nuptials. A fair number of them were from reporters. Allegra deleted those straightaway. The ones from curious acquaintances claiming to be sympathetic friends went into the trash, as well. After the deleting spree, only two messages remained, both from Talia.

Talia's first message was cryptic—"Call me. It's important." Allegra assumed she must have left something behind at her old apartment or somehow still owed Talia for part of last month's rent, even though she was fairly certain the financial matters were all squared away. Or maybe she, too, was calling about the nonwedding. She'd witnessed the spectacle firsthand after all.

Allegra completely missed the mark. Talia's second message was more forthcoming, and she never would have guessed the reason for the calls.

"Allegra, it's me again. Talia. One of the corps members in the traveling production has a stress fracture in her foot. She's pulled out of the tour, and we need someone. Everyone at the company knows about your, um, predicament. I think the director might be willing to give you the job. It's a very small part, even for a corps dancer. But if you're looking to get back into dance, it would be perfect. I know you could handle it. Call me!"

Allegra stared at the phone until the kitten in her arms meowed, snapping her back to reality.

She wasn't seriously thinking about going on tour with the ballet company, was she? She hadn't danced professionally in months.

Even if her body could handle the physical challenges, she wasn't sure it was the sort of plan she had in mind. Spots on the touring company were temporary. They only lasted as long as the tour. What would happen after the tour ended?

She'd be right back in the same position she was in right now. Minus the part about living in Zander's house, which should have been a definite plus.

The kitten meowed again and began to knead her paws on Allegra's leotard.

It's really not so terrible living here.

It wasn't terrible at all, actually. It was nice. So nice that it scared her. Which was precisely why Allegra couldn't bring herself to delete Talia's messages.

Three days later, Zander wasn't having a bit of luck getting the Vows reporter to take his calls. Despite Ryan's words of warning, he was surprised by his lack of headway. Freezing him out seemed like an extreme reaction, especially given the fact that he'd already been subjected to a scathing mention in the City section of New York's most widely read newspaper.

The way Zander saw it, he and Celestia Lane were even.

He'd been forced to implement plan B. If the reporter wouldn't come to the phone, he'd simply have to get in touch with her another way. Unfortunately, the options were severely limited.

Zander couldn't very well camp out at the *Times* building. That had *stalker* written all over it. Plus, it reeked of desperation. Since the most recent *Times* piece, the Bennington reservations desk had once again been inundated with wedding cancellations. So Zander was, in fact, desperate. But the reporter didn't need to know that.

An accidental meeting was the only option. If he bumped into the Vows columnist in a social setting, then maybe they could have a normal, pleasant conversation and she could see that he was actually a decent human being. At the very least, he wasn't some kind of marriage-hating monster at the helm of a cursed hotel. Brides weren't actually running away from the Bennington in droves. Then maybe, just maybe, they could agree to some sort of truce. If he never heard the word *curse* again, it would be too soon.

The idea might not be foolproof, but it was the only thing he'd managed to come up with.

The most obvious flaw in his plan had been the fact that he didn't have the first clue where he could bump into Celestia Lane. Lurking around the Starbucks closest to the *Times* building had seemed like a sure bet. Again, that was out of the question for reasons having to do with desperation.

The solution was obvious. Where was the one place he'd be sure to find a reporter who spent all her time writing about couples tying the knot? A wedding.

Zander hadn't exactly relished the idea of spending what little free time he had attending the nuptials of complete and total strangers. But alas, that was his current situation. Oh, how the mighty have fallen.

He'd been to three weddings in as many days. That was a lot of wedded bliss for anyone to take.

The one upside to his strange new hobby was that he hadn't set eyes on Allegra since the day he'd walked in on her dancing at his mother's school. And that was a good thing. A *very* good thing.

She'd been so beautiful he'd forgotten how to breathe. From the moment he entered the studio, he'd been rendered speechless. Motionless. A rush of desire like nothing he'd ever experienced had hit him hard and fast. If not for the ballet barre digging into his back, holding him upright, he would have fallen to his knees.

She was so graceful. So damn ethereal. Like something out of a dream. Yet he knew those curves. His hands were intimately familiar with her wisp of a waist and the warm dip of her lower back. He knew Allegra's body almost as well as he knew his own.

Watching her dance had awakened an urge he'd managed to ignore for the better part of his adult life. He wanted to dance again. He wanted to move with her, slowly and sweetly. He'd had to shove his hands into his pockets and clench his fists to stop himself from claiming his place beside her and pulling her into a dance hold.

Any hope he'd had of forgetting about the kiss they'd shared in the back seat of the Bennington limo evaporated then and there.

He wanted Allegra.

He wanted to know what her womanly curves felt like beneath his hands as he moved her across a dance floor. He wanted to taste her again, this time while her lithe legs wrapped around his hips as he drove himself inside her. He wanted her to cry his name while he watched her come apart.

The desire had been there all along. Zander had been consciously aware of it humming beneath the surface of his skin during each and every one of their interactions. Even when she'd stumbled into the ballroom and he'd stared at her as the candles dripped onto his cake. He'd pretty much been a goner since he'd let his gaze follow the trail of her wedding gown's tiny white buttons down the length of her supple spine. Which was wrong on multiple levels, but at least he'd been able to set it aside.

There'd been far too much history between them to act on his attraction. Far too many unanswered questions.

Plus the obvious complication that she'd been dressed in miles upon miles of white tulle at the time.

The kiss changed things.

He couldn't ignore his craving for her. Not anymore. He couldn't look at her without remembering what her lips felt like touching his. Too lovely. Too intimate. Like getting a glimpse into a secret, forbidden paradise.

Zander had never had such a visceral reaction to a kiss before.

But this was Allegra.

She was the one who got away, even if Zander's sixteen-year-old self had been too much of an idiot to tell her how he'd felt. She was also the one who seemed to be on the verge of some kind of emotional breakdown at the moment, and he'd waited far too long to stop her the other day in the limo.

Maybe he *was* a monster after all.

Distance.

That's what he needed.

Thank God for the weddings. While they'd been a colossal waste of time thus far, since the Vows reporter hadn't turned up at any of the three, they'd at least been an effective diversion. Usually, by the time Zander returned to the brownstone after a night of bouquet tossing and drunken toasts, Allegra had already gone to bed. The house was dark and quiet.

The night before, however, he could have sworn he heard a *meow* sound coming from Allegra's room. He'd paused outside her door and waited. And then… nothing.

He was losing it. He'd never had a cat in his life. Neither had his mother. So now he could add auditory hallucinations to his list of current problems.

Zander expected to find things at the brownstone the same when the Bennington limo dropped him off after the third wedding. But as he unfastened his bow tie and climbed up the front steps, he nearly tripped on something. He crouched down and realized it was a small saucer of what looked like dry cat food.

Interesting, especially in light of the meow.

He straightened and spotted Allegra standing in the shadows, just to the right of the porch's large marble columns. She wore a bathrobe pulled tight around her slender frame. Zander's eyes narrowed, adjusting to the darkness. He'd never seen the robe before. It was bubble gum pink. Hers, obviously.

It must have been one of the items in the overnight bag she'd finally recovered. Finding her in pajamas that weren't his shouldn't have bothered Zander.

But it did.

He cleared his throat and refocused his gaze on her face, pale and lovely in the moonlight. "Allegra."

"Zander." Her gaze flitted briefly to the small bowl at his feet. "Um, hi."

He bit back a smile. "It's awfully cold for a late-night walk, don't you think?"

She shrugged. "I couldn't sleep. Some fresh air seemed like a nice idea."

Her breath was a visible puff of vapor, mingling with his. "How was your date?" She cast a pointed glance at his tuxedo, visible through the unbuttoned opening of his overcoat.

"I haven't been on a date."

Would it bother you if I had?

"Oh. Sorry, I didn't mean to pry." Her cheeks

flushed pink in the darkness, until they were practically the color of her bathrobe.

She was cute when she was jealous.

Which was exactly the sort of thought he shouldn't be having. "It's okay. I was working late."

He didn't feel like going into the whole wedding-crasher thing. It was borderline pathetic and, thus far, wholly ineffective.

Besides, he didn't want to talk about work at the moment. Or weddings.

"Right." Allegra nodded absently and pulled at the tie of her robe.

She didn't believe him. Fine. Let her think he'd been running around Manhattan with a different woman on his arm every night this week. Did it really matter?

It matters. You know it does.

"It's late. We should probably get to bed." *We.* As if they were a couple.

What was he saying?

He was beginning to regret drinking that second glass of champagne at the nuptials of the newly christened Mr. and Mrs. Robert C. Williams. Whoever they were.

He turned toward the door.

"Wait." Allegra reached for his forearm with one hand, while the other kept a firm grip on her robe. "Can I ask you something? Please?"

Zander paused, much too aware of the press of her fingertips just above his wrist, even through multiple layers of clothing. "You can ask me anything, Allegra. Always."

"Why didn't you tell me you own the brownstone now?"

The question caught him off guard. He wasn't sure what he'd expected her to ask him after midnight on a snowy evening, but that wasn't it.

"Does it matter?" His words felt like they were coming from deep inside his chest somewhere, and his voice dropped an octave or two.

"Yes, it does. It matters because you let me tease you about living with your mother when it's the other way around. She invited me to stay here without telling you about it, and I know you weren't exactly excited about the idea." She removed her hand from his arm and took a deep breath. "I also understand why."

The snowflakes seemed to swirl in slow motion all of a sudden, and Zander felt like he was back inside the limo again…back to the moment just before she'd kissed him. He could almost feel the weight of her head on his shoulder, feel the warmth of her body nestled against his.

"Allegra." He gave his head a small shake.

They didn't need to do this. Not anymore. This conversation was taking place years too late.

"I left, Zander. I left, and you never heard from me again." Her voice trembled with something he couldn't quite identify.

Whatever it was sliced through him, leaving him raw. Bruised.

So they were going there, whether he wanted to or not.

Finally.

"I'm aware of the facts," he said, gritting his teeth.

Was he supposed to pretend he hadn't missed her? Or that he hadn't called a dozen times before he finally got the hint and gave up?

"And you still let me stay. Why?"

He swallowed. "Because it was the right thing to do."

"I see." She smiled, but her bottom lip wobbled just a little bit. Just enough to make Zander wish he'd told her the truth.

Because you belong here.

You always have, and you always will.

He sighed.

How had it come to this? Once upon a time, he'd been able to say anything to Allegra.

Almost anything, anyway.

He took a tense inhale and reminded himself he'd handled things as best he could. They'd been kids back then. She'd just lost her family. It wasn't the right time to tell her he'd fallen in love with her. Not when she was so vulnerable, so lost.

Since she'd come back, though, he'd begun to wonder…

Maybe it had been the perfect time to tell her how he felt. Maybe it had been just what she needed to hear in her darkest hours.

"Allegra…" He took a step closer.

Then he heard it again—a plaintive meow. It was unmistakable this time. Loud. Clear. And strangely enough, it seemed to be coming from inside Allegra's robe.

His gaze dropped to her chest. It meowed again.

Zander's eyes moved back to her face, which was flushing furiously now. "Why do I get the feeling I've got another houseguest?"

She loosened her robe, and a tiny feline face peered

at Zander from behind thick pink terry cloth. "This isn't how it looks."

He arched an eyebrow. "You mean you don't actually have a kitten hidden in your bathrobe right now?"

"I do." Allegra bit her lip. Then she extricated the kitten from her clothes and let it burrow into the crook of her elbow, where it gave Zander the most pitiful look it could muster. "She's just a stray that I'm looking after. She's definitely not mine."

Zander's lips twitched into a grin. "Does the cat realize that?"

"I felt sorry for her, so I brought her inside. I heard her meowing out here a little while ago, so I came to get her again."

"What's her name?"

"I haven't given her one. I told you, she's just a stray." Allegra held the kitten tighter to her chest. "She was out here in the cold, all alone."

"We can't have that now, can we?" He ran a hand over the cat's soft head, and she purred, pushing her tiny cheek against his fingertips.

"No, we can't."

There it was again. *We.*

Their eyes met, and Zander could have sworn he was looking at the girl he'd danced with all those years ago, the girl she'd been before the day of their last recital.

Happy.

Whole.

"You can stay here as long as you like, Allegra." The night had gone soft and quiet, and his voice was a hoarse whisper in the dark. "Your nameless kitten, too."

Just...

Stay.

"Thank you." Allegra's bottom lip slid slowly between her teeth. "But she's really not mine. I'm only taking care of her. It's temporary."

Of course it was.

This wasn't a reunion. It was a respite. Allegra was only biding her time, trying to figure things out until she said goodbye.

Zander had nearly forgotten.

"Understood." He nodded. "Good night to you both, then."

And as he climbed the silent stairs of the old brownstone, he couldn't help but wonder—would there be a goodbye this time, or would she slip away again?

In the end, was there really a difference? He used to think so. Now he wasn't so sure.

Chapter Nine

The idea came to Allegra right at the end of preballet class on Friday morning.

She'd just led the class of twelve or so four-year-olds through the reverence, somehow suppressing a grin at their adorably wobbly curtsies. Then Allegra concluded the class by giving each little girl a tight hug, a tradition she loved and dreaded in equal parts because it always left her with a lump in her throat.

Her students were so innocent, so untouched by the cruelty of the world in their pink tights and tiny ballet slippers. Sometimes she had to focus on the wall behind their heads when she wrapped her arms around their slender little shoulders instead of looking them in the eyes.

Today was one of those times.

Still, she hugged each and every tiny dancer and

whispered words of encouragement as they filed out of the studio door. *Great work today! See you Monday.*

"I love you, Miss Allegra," one of the girls mumbled into her shoulder.

Allegra's breath caught in her throat.

Don't get attached.

"Have a nice weekend, Lily," she said, shifting her gaze from the girl's springy red curls to the lobby wall.

The recital photos still hung there, of course. Allegra had gotten used to them now, though. She'd grown accustomed to the wave of nostalgia that washed over her when she studied them, even when she let her gaze linger a little too long on the photograph of her and Zander.

This time, her attention snagged on one of the older pictures. She walked closer and stared at it as her students threw themselves at the mothers, fathers and nannies in the waiting area—a ritual even more excruciating than the end-of-class hug.

The photograph was black-and-white, and unlike the other pictures, which were mostly posed recital keepsakes, this one looked like a candid shot. The couple in the foreground faced the camera in an open swing-dance hold, while dozens of other pairs spun dizzying circles behind them. All the dancers had numbers pinned to their backs, leading Allegra to believe the picture had been taken at a ballroom dance competition like the ones she and Zander had entered back in the day.

But up close she realized that didn't seem quite right. The couples in the photo weren't as slick and polished as competition dancers typically were, even the novices. Their wide smiles and sharp kicks had a joyful, almost manic feel.

Allegra angled her head, examined the photo for another second or two, then plucked it off the wall and carried it to Emily's office. "Is this photo what I think it is?"

Emily looked up from the costume catalog spread open on her desk and smiled. "That depends. If you're wondering if the couple up front and center are my parents, then yes. You're correct."

Allegra studied the smiling man and woman in the black-and-white image again. If they were Emily's parents, that made them Zander's grandparents. She could see it now. The man in the picture had the same broad shoulders, the same soulful eyes as Zander.

Her throat grew tight thinking about the way those eyes had looked at her the night before on the steps of the brownstone. Like he wasn't merely tolerating her presence but enjoying it. Like he wanted her to stay.

He'd been so sweet to the kitten, too. So gentle.

She couldn't keep the cat, no matter how very badly she wanted to. She might have a bed to sleep in and a roof over her head for the moment, but she couldn't stay at the brownstone forever. That would be crazy.

Allegra swallowed.

If staying in New York was crazy, why hadn't she returned Talia's call yet?

Living here permanently hadn't sounded crazy when Zander suggested it. He'd made it sound almost normal. Almost…*nice.*

You can stay here as long as you like, Allegra. Your nameless kitten, too.

Of course by the end of the conversation he'd looked

as if he wanted to take it back. His face had gone back to being as blank as a slate.

"I can't believe I never knew these were your parents. Zander never said anything." Allegra peered at the smiling man and woman in the black-and-white image. "But this wasn't taken at a dance competition, was it?"

Emily shook her head. "Good eye. No, it wasn't. Care to take a guess?"

"It's a dance marathon, isn't it?"

"Bingo." Emily beamed. "They were quite popular back in the day. I think that photo was taken in 1942. Maybe 1943. My mother and father were newly engaged and determined to be the last remaining couple on the dance floor so they could win the grand-prize money. My mom had her heart set on a society wedding at the Plaza, and the couple who danced the longest that night won three thousand dollars."

"That had to be a fortune back then. Did they win? Did your mother get her dream wedding?" Allegra hoped so.

Emily reached across her desk for the framed photograph and ran her fingertips lovingly over the picture. "They did. They danced for twenty-seven hours and fourteen minutes straight. Three months later, they said 'I do.'"

"At the Plaza?"

"No." Emily let out a laugh. "Believe it or not they got married at the Bennington."

"You're kidding." Zander's grandparents had exchanged vows at his hotel decades before he worked there? For some reason, that struck Allegra as outrageously romantic. Which was something of a shock, considering romance was the absolute last thing on her mind.

Along with weddings.

And Zander Wilde.

She took a deep breath. This conversation wasn't supposed to have anything to do with the past. Or romance. It was supposed to be about moving on. Plus one very important thing—money.

"Isn't there a college somewhere in the Midwest that holds a dance marathon once a year as a fund-raiser for their marching band?"

Allegra remembered reading about the event in a dance magazine a while back. The band members played old swing standards, songs from Glenn Miller and Benny Goodman, while students danced until they dropped. The annual event had become so popular that the most recent marathon had raised enough money for the band to buy all new instruments.

"I think you're right," Emily said, handing the picture back to Allegra. "Can you imagine how much fun something like that would be?"

"I can. And I'm glad you like the idea because I think we should have one." Allegra could already see it—streamers and retro bunting, a disco ball hanging from the ceiling. So perfectly retro. So perfectly *perfect.* "We could charge a modest entry fee, plus the couples could get supporters to pledge money for each hour they spend on the dance floor. We could give away a trophy to the winners, both the couple who lasts the longest and the dancers who raise the most money. All the funds could go to the school."

It could work.

If it did, maybe the school would get enough of

a bump to put it into the black. The money from the sale of the brownstone wouldn't last forever, and while Zander was obviously quite successful, he couldn't support the Wilde School of Dance indefinitely. Especially when brides were running away from his hotel in droves.

Allegra still felt a little responsible for the mess Zander was in. Okay, *a lot* responsible.

She kept telling herself the "curse" wasn't her fault. After all, she wasn't the *only* runaway bride.

Still. She'd been the most recent one. The most notorious one, apparently. And the *Times* wasn't backing down.

The damage was done. It was obviously too late for her to do anything about the curse, but maybe she could help Emily's school.

"It sounds wonderful. I love the idea, especially since it ties in with the Wilde family history. But I'm not sure I can pull off something like that on my own. I suppose Tessa and Chloe might be able to help."

"No need. I'll do it." It was the least Allegra could do after everything Emily had done for her. After everything she was *still* doing.

It's Zander's house, remember? It's his bed you're sleeping in.

She released a shaky breath. "If you like the idea, let me put together a dance marathon. I can get something planned quickly enough. We could probably get a lot of nice word of mouth just in time for class registration for the new semester."

The more Allegra thought about it, the better her idea seemed. They could raise some money and increase the size of their enrollment at the same time. It was win-win.

Of course if she committed to putting together a fund-raiser, she'd have to stick around long enough to see it through. Effectively, she'd be choosing to stay on as a teacher at the school. At least for another week or two.

But she could do that, couldn't she? She'd still have time to sign on for the ballet tour…

Maybe.

But that would require calling the ballet director or, at the very least, Talia. So far Allegra hadn't come close to contacting either of them.

"I'd hate to impose on you like that, dear," Emily said.

"It's the least I can do. I don't know where I would be right now if you hadn't helped me the night of the wedding. A dance marathon really wouldn't be too hard to put together." Allegra should know. She'd spent more time than she liked to admit helping organize campaign events for Spencer. Because that's what perfect political wives did instead of languishing on the bottom rung of a third-tier ballet company. Or so she'd been told.

She shuddered to think how close she'd come to making that her life, all for a man who'd been cheating on her. A man she wasn't sure she'd ever actually loved.

She was better off alone. Allegra was used to life on her own. It was better this way.

Predictable.

Safe.

Zander's image flitted briefly through her consciousness. His perfectly square jaw. His hands. His mouth.

A shiver coursed through her that felt anything but safe and predictable.

Something was wrong with her. Obviously. She had to get over this ridiculous infatuation she'd somehow developed with regard to her oldest friend.

Concentrate. You've got a fund-raiser to plan. "The most difficult part would be finding a location. After that, the rest should fall into place easily."

Emily shrugged. "We could always have it here at the school."

Allegra nodded. "We could. But I was thinking someplace bigger. Someplace special, so we could draw more people. I already have a few ideas in mind."

Technically, she only had one place in mind. But it was perfect, and she was almost certain she'd be able to pull it off.

"You really want to take this on?" Emily asked.

"I do." Allegra nodded.

This would be good. Not just for the school, but for her, as well. She clearly needed something to occupy her thoughts.

Something other than kissing Zander Wilde.

Another day, another wedding.

Zander still hadn't managed to get any face time with the Vows reporter, but he had high hopes for Friday night.

The midweek ceremonies had been long shots. He knew that. Most couples chose to get married on the weekend, particularly the kind of high-profile brides and grooms who were regularly featured on the wedding pages in the *Times*. Still, he had to try.

While his failure to cross paths with Celestia Lane

earlier in the week had been disappointing, Zander didn't consider it cause for alarm. Tonight was a different story.

Vows would run again in the Sunday edition. This was it. Tonight was his last chance to make a favorable impression on Ms. Lane before she once again offered up her thoughts on the Manhattan wedding scene for everyone in the city to read over weekend brunch. He needed the Bennington to be included in those thoughts. Favorably, if at all possible.

After a meticulous investigation that involved combing through the past three months' issues of *Vogue*, *Vanity Fair* and *Town & Country*, as well as a ridiculous number of hours poring over Page Six, Zander was certain he and Ryan had identified the wedding that would be splashed across the Vows headline this weekend.

The bride was a fashion stylist whose clients regularly appeared on the pages of the *Times*'s Lifestyle section, and the groom was a junior partner at one of the biggest law firms in the city's financial district. Both the ceremony and the reception were to take place at the Museum of Natural History, which—according to a rumor that had been repeated no less than four times in Page Six alone—was being lavishly decorated in a secret-garden theme. If the rumor was true, wedding guests would be treated to a three-course meal in the Milstein Hall of Ocean Life, in the shadow of the museum's iconic blue whale, surrounded by peonies and terrariums of succulents.

Zander couldn't have cared less about the plants. Or the meal. Or the whale. But he cared very much about the fact that the wedding was being hailed as the social event of the season.

Celestia Lane's appearance was a certainty.

So was Zander's.

He had the driver drop him off a block from the museum and walked the rest of the way down Central Park West. Best to forgo taking his car and using the valet in case they kept a guest list, because yes, he was still technically crashing.

Zander considered that a minor point, though, because he had no intention of going anywhere near the actual ceremony and reception. He knew better than to fake an invite to an event where every paparazzo in Manhattan would be in attendance. All he had to do was bump into the Vows reporter in the lobby. The museum was a big place, but it only had one main entrance. He'd imply he was there for a meeting of some sort, turn on the charm and, with any luck at all, get another dinner scheduled.

It was the best he could hope for.

The wedding was scheduled to begin at six o'clock, just fifteen minutes after the museum closed. Thank God. It was a small enough window to make his meeting excuse plausible.

The sun had just begun to dip below the New York skyline when Zander made his way toward the steps of the massive building. The stone figures atop the museum's Gothic columns were covered with a soft blanket of snow, and the sky darkened from blue to violet overhead.

Zander hesitated as he reached for the door. How long had it been since he'd set foot inside this iconic building?

A while.

Fourteen years, minimum.

He withdrew his hand, shoved it into the pocket of his overcoat and took a backward step.

This had been their place. His and Allegra's. They'd spent nearly as much time between the museum's hallowed walls as they had at dance practice.

As chairman of the museum's board, her father had retained an office right upstairs. It was in one of the Gothic building's turrets, which had delighted Allegra to no end. She'd once told Zander that when she'd been very small, she'd thought the museum was a castle. Her father's kingdom.

However, Zander could count the number of times he'd actually seen Preston Clark behind the desk of his exquisite turret office on one hand. Allegra's father spent most of his time in his law office on Park Avenue.

But that hadn't stopped Allegra from dragging Zander to the museum every spare moment they had. On the rare occasions when dance class ended early or was canceled altogether, they'd grab a burger at the diner around the corner from the studio and then head uptown. Zander hadn't needed to ask where they were going. It was a given.

Likewise, every one of Allegra's birthday parties took place at the museum. Long before Zander knew her well enough to complete nearly all her sentences, he'd labored under the misconception that she was just oddly passionate about dinosaurs. But it wasn't the bones that drew her there time and again. She'd been searching for something else.

Preston Clark rarely turned up to watch Allegra dance at the school's yearly recital. Zander couldn't recall the man spending more than five minutes at any of those birthday parties at the museum. If he couldn't be bothered to spend time in his daughter's world, she'd been determined to come into his.

Zander clenched his fists in the pockets of his overcoat. A lot of years had passed, but time hadn't erased the memory of the hurt in Allegra's eyes every time she'd peered past the red velvet curtain on recital evenings and seen empty seats in the audience where her parents should have been. Time hadn't made the bitter irony of the fact that their fatal accident had occurred on their way to watch her dance any easier to swallow.

They'd been on their way. Finally.

Allegra blamed herself, of course. "It's all my fault," she'd whispered, again and again, as Zander held her that night.

He knew it was wrong to hate a dead man, but Zander had never been so angry with anyone in his life as he'd been at Allegra's father in the agonizing hours that followed.

He still was, he realized, as he stared up at the museum's towering facade.

None of that mattered now, though. He hadn't come here to chase ghosts. He was here to save his business, and he couldn't do that while he was standing on the top step, gazing at his reflection in the glass double doors, imagining he was seeing a teenage kid instead of the man he'd become.

People were passing him now. Men in black tie and women in long beaded gowns were murmuring words like *pardon* and *sorry* while they stepped in front of him and entered the building. Wedding guests.

Get ahold of yourself, for crying out loud. You have a job to do.

Zander pulled the door open and stepped inside.

He glanced up at the violet light filtering through the rotunda, bathing the great room in winter's soft hues. Then he swallowed hard and forced himself to look past the two looming dinosaur skeletons, locked in eternal battle while New York's glittering elite sparkled at their feet. He swept the room with his gaze, searching for a glimpse of the Vows columnist. He'd studied the head shot beside her byline long enough to recognize her anywhere.

Just when he was on the verge of giving up, he saw her. She was walking straight toward him through the throng of people, her brow furrowed in confusion as she spotted him.

To say Zander was surprised as well would have been an understatement, although in a way it made sense. Perfect sense, because the woman walking toward him wasn't Celestia Lane.

It was Allegra.

Chapter Ten

Allegra didn't question Zander's sudden appearance at the museum at first. On some level, she wasn't the least bit surprised to find him standing in the lobby after her meeting with the event planner. She felt like she'd been looking over her shoulder for a glimpse of him since the moment she'd stepped through the building's familiar columned entryway.

Which was silly, really. Why should Zander be at the Museum of Natural History on a random Friday night? This was the present, not the past. They weren't children anymore.

Yet there he was, dressed in one of his impeccably cut suits with his smoldering gaze fixed unwaveringly on hers as she crossed the room toward him.

Her breathing grew increasingly shallow with each

click of her stilettos on the mosaic tile floor. What *was* he doing here, anyway?

She gazed up at him. He was a good three or four inches taller than she was, even in her heels. The last time she'd been so close to him in this same spot, they'd stood eye to eye. So much had changed.

Has it, though? Has it really?

"Zander." She swallowed. "You're here."

"Indeed I am." He cast a glance at the crowd of elegantly dressed people spilling through the museum's doors.

When his gaze flitted back to Allegra, her stomach gave an annoying little flip. "I'm confused. What's going on?"

Had Emily told him where to find her?

No, that couldn't be it. Allegra had told her she had an appointment to talk to someone about a location for the dance marathon, but she very purposefully hadn't breathed a word about the museum. She didn't want to promise something until she was 100 percent sure she could deliver.

As it turned out, she couldn't.

Her father's name was engraved on a memorial plaque in the museum's turret offices, and an exhibition in one of the galleries had been named after him "in gratitude for over a decade of service." Almost everyone in the event-planning department remembered Allegra and had kind things to say about her father, but that was where the special treatment ended. The museum's schedule was packed for the next year and a half. The soonest they could accommodate the dance marathon would be the middle of next year, and even then, Allegra would be expected to pay the full going rate.

"You first," Zander said. "What are you doing here?"

"I had a meeting. It was disastrous." She tilted her head. "You?"

"I'm here for a wedding." Zander clenched his jaw. "Sort of."

"Sort of?" Allegra lifted an eyebrow.

How did a person *sort of* attend a wedding?

"Correct. Sort of." Again, his gaze darted toward the flow of guests moving from the glass double doors toward the Milstein Hall of Ocean Life.

"Oh, my God." Allegra let out a laugh and then dropped her voice to a conspiratorial whisper. "You're crashing, aren't you?"

"No." The corner of Zander's mouth quirked into a grin. "Okay, yes. But not the actual reception. I'm only lingering at the cocktail hour to see if I can find the reporter who keeps writing about the curse in the *Times*."

Again with the curse.

Things at Zander's hotel must be a lot worse than he'd been letting on.

"You're just going to pretend you're a guest and ambush her here in the lobby?"

Zander's eyes narrowed. "Do you have a better suggestion?"

Allegra looked him up and down. "It'll never work. You should have brought a date. She'll never buy the fact that Zander Wilde, bachelor at large, would go to something like this by himself."

Half the women in Manhattan would have probably leaped at the chance to crash a wedding with him.

She wondered why one of those women wasn't

standing beside him right now. Then she wondered why she cared. Or why his dateless status somehow took the edge off her disappointment over her unsuccessful meeting.

"I suppose you have a point." Zander glanced at the Cartier timepiece strapped around his wrist and frowned. "Any other advice? Perhaps something I can actually put into practice in the next five minutes or so?"

"You might have sent a gift for appearance purposes." She shrugged. "A toaster, maybe?"

"Again, not helpful. Unless you've got something from Sur La Table in that giant bag of yours?" He clenched his jaw again, and this time a rather fascinating knot formed in his chiseled jaw.

"Nope. Just pointe shoes."

Zander's eyes darkened a shade. Then his gaze dropped to her mouth and lingered for a moment or two. Just long enough for Allegra's knees to go a little wobbly. "Just pointe shoes. That's a shame, now, isn't it?"

There was an edge to his tone that sounded suspiciously flirtatious. Allegra wondered what it would be like to dance for him, to wind pink satin ribbons around her ankles and lose herself in a song. For real this time, not just for a few bars of music.

Just for Zander.

"I should go," she blurted.

"Right." The heat in Zander's fierce dark eyes cooled slightly. He nodded toward the Hall of Ocean Life, where music had begun to swell. "The cocktail hour has already started. I'm running out of time."

"Okay, then." Allegra's feet stubbornly refused to move. "I guess I'll see you later at home."

That word again. *Home.*

She rose up on tiptoe and pressed a chaste kiss to Zander's cheek. He smelled so good, so familiar, that her fingertips lingered on the smooth satin lapels of his tuxedo and her lips hovered near the corner of his mouth for just a moment too long.

Then Zander's hands were suddenly sliding from her waist to the center of her back, holding her in place.

Allegra squeezed her eyes shut. *Leave now. Leave while you still can.*

"You could stay, you know," Zander murmured. "You could pretend to be my date for this thing, since I apparently need one."

She pulled back slightly, searching his gaze. Was he serious?

He arched an eyebrow. "Unless you're in a hurry to get back to the brownstone to feed that sad little cat of yours."

Allegra's response was automatic. "She's not my cat."

Zander shrugged one shoulder. "Then I'm assuming you're free."

She was. But was it really a good idea to stay and crash a wedding with Zander?

It's not an actual date. The whole evening is just pretend.

Still, she wasn't staying.

Absolutely not.

She smiled up at him. "Lead the way."

Zander wasn't sure exactly when it happened, but at some point during the course of the evening, he stopped scanning the faces of the posh crowd, hoping to a catch a glimpse of Celestia Lane.

Maybe it was sometime around his second martini. Or was the chilled glass currently in his hand his third?

No telling.

The only thing he knew for certain was he'd needed something to take the edge off when Allegra slipped her hand in his as they'd entered the iconic gallery.

The bride and groom weren't messing around with their secret-garden theme. The room had been completely transformed. The great blue whale still loomed overhead, and the customary ocean-life exhibits flanked the immense space as always. But a mass of wisteria and wispy vines hung suspended from the ceiling, creating an enchanted forest. The glass display cases glowed bright blue in the dimly lit room, giving the atmosphere a mysterious, otherworldly feel.

It was like crossing a threshold and stepping into the Garden of Eden. His head spun, and certain other body parts took note, as well.

Adam and Eve...

Zander and Allegra.

So yes, a cocktail had been a very necessary diversion, because Zander could feel himself slipping away, falling under the spell of the lush surroundings.

Still, he was perfectly sober and he knew it. It wasn't the alcohol that made him forget that he and Allegra weren't on a real date—it was the way she tipped her head back when she laughed at something he said. It was the gentle weight of her fingertips resting on his forearm, even when no one seemed to be paying them any attention. It was the room itself—wild and heavy with the scent of orchids and memories.

He felt like they were on a real date, no matter how many times he reminded himself they weren't.

His gaze slid toward Allegra standing beside him, sipping from a slender champagne flute. She'd just finished a fifteen-minute conversation with the bride's sister and, due to Allegra's connection to the museum, managed to secure an actual invitation for them both to stay for the reception. Zander was fairly certain the two women had exchanged cell numbers. So much for flying under the radar. "Having fun?"

"Very much, actually." She searched his gaze and pulled a face. "Relax. You look far too serious. Going to a stranger's wedding isn't the sort of thing you can do halfway. In order to be believable, you need to go all in."

"Remind me again how many times you've done this."

"Zero." She shrugged. "But I've seen my fair share of Vince Vaughn movies. Face it. You know I'm right. Just like I was right when I said you needed a date. Otherwise I wouldn't be standing next to you right now."

She had a point.

She'd been onto something when she insisted he needed a date. He just wasn't 100 percent sure that was why he'd asked her to stay.

"So it's not uncomfortable for you, being around all this?" He gestured toward the cake table, where the bride and groom were currently engaged in the age-old tradition of smashing icing into each other's face.

Ah, romance, Zander thought wryly.

Allegra sipped her champagne, tilted her head and considered the couple. "Oddly enough, no. My own wedding feels like it was a million years ago. It was a mistake—one that I won't be repeating ever again."

"Never?" Zander's chest tightened. Just a bit.

She gave her head a definitive shake. "Never. I've realized I'm not the marrying type."

He narrowed his gaze but suppressed his nonsensical urge to argue. *Why do you care?* "So you're going to live happily ever after with your nameless cat?"

"Yes." She blinked. "I mean, no. Because she's not my cat."

He smiled into his martini. "Sure she's not."

Allegra cleared her throat. "Don't judge. You're practically allergic to this whole scene."

Zander lifted his gaze, but she was suddenly focusing intently on a dolphin diorama that he was certain she'd seen hundreds of times before. "What makes you say that?"

She glanced at him and gave him a thorough once-over. "For one, you look distinctly uncomfortable right now."

Probably because he'd only sort of been invited to this shindig. But also because the conversation had taken a somewhat dangerous turn.

"Second, you nearly had a heart attack at your birthday party when you thought I wanted to marry you." She smiled sweetly at him. Too sweetly. "You have *bachelor* written all over you."

He stared at her for a beat. The teasing smile on her lips began to look a little strained around the edges.

She set down her champagne glass on a nearby cocktail table. "Sorry, Zander. I..."

"I had a wedding, too, once, you know." The words

were out of his mouth before he could stop them. *Damn it.*

She grew very still. Her eyes were suddenly huge in her face. As big as saucers. "No, I didn't know. And now I feel even worse."

"Don't. It was a near miss, just like yours." He smiled, but it felt forced, and he knew better than to hope she didn't notice.

They couldn't hide from one another anymore. Not here. Too much had happened between these walls. And now here they were again, only this time it was different. *They* were different.

Zander was tired of trying to forget the heat simmering between them since they'd kissed. Tired of fighting his desire when he knew good and well she felt it, too.

"When was this?" she whispered.

He exhaled a tense breath. "Around two years ago."

Had it been that recently? He supposed it had.

Zander had walked away from the church that day and never looked back, knowing with absolute certainty he'd done the right thing.

When he'd proposed, he'd fully intended to go through with the wedding. Obviously. He'd *wanted* to marry Laura. He thought he had, anyway.

But as the wedding date had drawn near, he'd been unable to shake the memory of his deal with Allegra.

Let's make a deal. If neither of us is married by the time we turn thirty, we'll marry each other. Agreed?

Agreed.

The idea that she might return to New York one day tormented him. What if she came home alone and found him married?

What if…

He ground his teeth together. Could he possibly have been more idiotic? He'd called off his wedding because of doubts—doubts based, in part, on a memory that Allegra had no recollection of whatsoever.

"It's in the past," he said.

Like so much else.

She nodded, but the look in her eyes just about killed him. As if she understood more than what he was willing to admit. As if she *knew.*

A waiter carrying a tray of fizzy champagne flutes stopped in front of them? "Another drink, sir?"

God, yes.

"Thank you." Zander exchanged his empty martini glass for one of the slender flutes. He took a sip but barely tasted it. Allegra was still watching him in a way that turned him inside out.

"Tell me about your disastrous meeting," he said, simply to change the subject. "Why are you at the museum on a Friday night, dressed to kill?"

His first guess had been a job interview, which he found intensely alarming for some strange reason. She seemed to like being back at the studio.

"I'm planning a fund-raiser for the dance school," she said.

Zander ignored the twinge of relief that this news prompted.

She wasn't going anywhere.

Yet.

"What kind of fund-raiser?"

Her smile brightened. "A retro dance marathon, like the one from the picture of your grandparents on the wall in the studio. Doesn't that sound perfect?"

"It does." Zander hadn't thought about that picture

in years, and now Allegra was apparently planning an entire fund-raiser around it.

It was indeed perfect. Fitting. Meaningful. And like everything else about Allegra, steeped in the past.

"I hoped we could have it here, but the calendar is full for the next year and a half. I can't wait that long."

"When did you have in mind?"

"Ten days from now, in time for next semester's registration." Her gaze shifted away from him.

As she focused on the bride, Zander couldn't quite shake the feeling there was more to her urgency than the new semester.

She's already got one foot out the door.

A muscle in his jaw tensed. "Have it at the Bennington."

Allegra's gaze flew back to his. "Seriously?"

"Why not? Our ballroom is just sitting there empty, remember?"

Which was precisely why he was attending this wedding reception in the first place. Why was he having so much trouble remembering that crucial fact?

"Thank you." Allegra beamed. "I'll handle everything. You won't need to be involved at all."

"Great," he said tersely.

He was just about to remind her that the school belonged to his mother, and he'd be more than willing to throw in some simple catering and a live band, but before he could, the bride's sister came swishing back in their direction in her billowy bridesmaid dress.

"Allegra!" She hugged her like she'd rediscovered a long-lost friend. "Come on. It's time for the bouquet toss."

"Um." Allegra shook her head. Vehemently. "I'm going to sit that out."

"Don't be silly. It'll be fun." The sister hooked her arm through Allegra's, apparently intent on dragging her along with her toward the crowd of women assembling on the dance floor.

"No, really. Zander and I were in the middle of discussing something, anyway. Weren't we?" Allegra cast a pleading glance at him as Beyoncé's "Single Ladies (Put a Ring on It)" blared from the loudspeakers.

He bit back a smile. "You just said I didn't need to be involved at all. Remember?"

She shot him a murderous glare.

"Best of luck, darling." He bent to kiss her cheek and whispered, "Weren't you just lecturing me about going all in?"

"I'm going to strangle you," she muttered under her breath.

"Don't worry. I'm sure you won't catch it since you're never getting married." He winked.

The sister gave her arm a final tug. Within seconds, Allegra was on the dance floor, pushing other women in front of her in a desperate attempt to wiggle her way to the back of the crowd of single ladies.

The bride started counting backward from ten.

"Ten, nine, eight..."

Allegra crossed her arms, glowered at Zander and mouthed, "You're dead."

"...seven, six, five..."

Zander waved at her. For possibly the first time since the night of his birthday, he had the upper hand. Every interaction with Allegra seemed to leave him feeling off balance and unsatisfied in ways he didn't care to think about. It felt good to be the one in control again.

"…four, three, two…"

He set down his drink and headed toward the spectacle. He'd never planned on forcing Allegra to really go through with it. He only wanted to rattle her a little bit. Tease her, just like old times. Then he'd swoop in at the last minute and escort her away from the fray where they could have a good laugh over it.

But as Zander crossed the room, a sense of unease knotted in his chest. What if she wasn't as fine with being at a wedding as she'd indicated? He didn't want to prompt another panic attack. What was he thinking?

"…one!"

Zander hastened his steps, but just as he reached the edge of the dance floor, the bridal bouquet went airborne. He lunged to wrap an arm around Allegra's waist and pull her close, but he was too late.

The bundle of white flowers sailed past his head and landed with a thud in the arms of a stunned Allegra.

Chapter Eleven

Allegra's first instinct was to drop the bouquet.

So she did.

She simply let go of it and watched it fall to the floor as if she was playing a game of hot potato. Right away, someone let out a gasp. Allegra wasn't sure who.

A moment of shocked silence followed. Allegra could feel her heartbeat in her throat. She'd just thrown the bridal bouquet to the ground. How could she possibly explain this behavior? Never mind that. How would she explain her presence at this fancy party when the bride realized she wasn't an actual wedding guest, but only a very, very new friend of the bride's sister?

Do something.

Everyone was staring at her, which was only making things worse.

She bent to pick up the flowers and kept her gaze

glued to the elegant little pile of white peonies and garden roses at her feet. Somewhere in the periphery, she heard a voice call out, "Get it!"

And then all hell broke loose.

One of the bridesmaids dived toward the bouquet. Then another. And another. A few of the guests followed suit, until the scene looked more like something that should be going down on the five-yard line of a football field than at a wedding reception.

Allegra stood and stared, not quite believing what she was seeing.

"Let's get out of here," a low voice rumbled beside her.

She blinked, snapping out of her trance.

Zander.

His firm hand wrapped around her wrist, and she was consciously aware of her pulse booming against the pad of his thumb.

She nodded and stepped away from the chaos.

Zander cut a quick path through the cheering guests, and Allegra followed him. She wasn't entirely sure where they were going, but she didn't care. She just wanted to get away from the bouquet before she got stuck with it again…or worse. What if the wedding photographer wanted to take her picture? Blending in at a wedding reception was one thing. A total stranger appearing prominently in someone's wedding album was another.

Zander led her past the cake table and through the maze of white chairs and wild orchid centerpieces, back to the lobby, now quiet and empty since the party was in full swing.

Allegra took a deep breath. They were safe.

Her head spun a little. The sudden silence was disorienting after being at the noisy reception. Their footsteps on the mosaic floor seemed far too loud. Allegra's senses were on high alert. She could hear every little sound—the rustle of Zander's tuxedo jacket, the swish of her skirt, her breath coming hard and fast.

Zander paused, scrubbed a hand over his face and shook his head. "You caught the bouquet."

"No, I didn't." She shook her head. "Well, I did. But then it fell, so it didn't actually count."

The corner of his mouth tugged into a half grin. "That's not how it looked from where I was standing."

"Maybe you weren't paying attention."

"Oh, I was definitely paying attention. You threw those flowers at the ground like they were on fire." He lifted an accusatory brow.

Mr. Runaway Groom thought it was funny, did he?

"Maybe we should go back inside for the garter toss and see how you'd react if you ended up with it?" She spun on her heel and marched back toward the reception.

Zander caught her elbow. And then his hand slid slowly down her arm until their fingertips were intertwined. Their laughter grew quiet.

Allegra stood very still, almost afraid to turn around and face him. *Don't be ridiculous. It's only Zander.*

There was nothing to be afraid of. He was her friend.

But there was nothing friendly about the chill that coursed through her when he touched her this time. Nothing friendly at all. From the heavy thud of her heart to the delicious little flutter low in her belly, she felt alive in a way that both thrilled and frightened her.

She shouldn't be feeling this way around him.

Overwhelmed by his presence.

He filled up the room, every corner of the cavernous space. It defied logic, but she could sense him all around her. Not just beside her, but in the air itself.

She spun around, convinced she was only imagining the heat that seemed to flow from his fingertips to hers. She wasn't. It was in his gaze, too, in the way his eyes swept over her, almost as if he was seeing her for the very first time.

The wonder in his expression was so reverent—so new, yet at the same time so very much Zander—that it nearly made her cry.

Her gaze dropped to his mouth. God help her, she wanted to kiss him again. Only this time she couldn't blame her desire on feeling fuzzy and disoriented. She couldn't even blame it on nostalgia, because as much as she loved the comfort of his familiarity, she craved the newness of him more.

The square cut of his jaw intrigued her, as did the hard, broad expanse of his chest. He was so big. So solid. So very much a man now.

She'd spent quite some time wondering what it would feel like to slip her hands beneath his shirt and explore the taut muscles of his abdomen. To feel the masculine heat of his body and marvel at how very much it had changed over the years.

She swallowed.

Allegra didn't know where to look. She was convinced he could read her mind, and the thought mortified her to the core.

Her gaze shifted to the glass double doors. Beyond them, snowflakes danced against the darkened sky and the lights of Manhattan glittered like gemstones spilled onto black velvet. She'd forgotten how beautiful the city could be at this time of year. She'd forgotten so very much.

"We should probably get going now," she murmured in a voice that didn't sound at all like herself. She sounded hoarse and breathy. Desperate.

Zander's eyes narrowed. "Is that what you want?"

No. It wasn't at all what she wanted.

She couldn't bear to tell him that she wanted to feel him again—his lips, his tongue, his hands. The last time they'd kissed hadn't ended well. She had no desire to repeat that kind of embarrassment.

But she couldn't force the words out either. Zander knew her too well. She couldn't look him in the eye and tell him she wanted to go home.

Is that what you want? The question was still there, in his eyes. All she had to do was decide.

She took a deep breath and shook her head.

Zander leaned closer, his eyes hard on hers. Then he reached to cup her face with his free hand, drawing the pad of his thumb, slowly, deliberately, along the swell of her bottom lip. "Tell me what you want, Allegra."

You. She swallowed. *I want you.*

"This," she said, reaching up on tiptoe to close the space between them and touch her lips to his.

What are you doing? Stop.

But it was too late to change her mind. Too late to pretend she didn't want this. Because the moment her mouth grazed Zander's, he took ownership of the kiss.

His hands slid into her hair, holding her in place, while his tongue slid brazenly along the seam of her lips until they parted, opening for him.

Then there was nothing but heat and want and the

shocking reality that this was what she'd wanted all along. Zander.

Had she always felt this way? It seemed impossible. Yet beneath the newness of his mouth on hers and the crush of her breasts against the solid wall of his chest, there was something else. A feeling she couldn't quite put her finger on. A sense of belonging. Of destiny.

Home.

Allegra squeezed her eyes closed. She didn't want to imagine herself fitting into this life again. There was too much at stake. Too much to lose. But no matter how hard she railed against it, there it was, shimmering before like her a mirage.

She whimpered into Zander's mouth, and he groaned in return, gently guiding her backward until her spine was pressed against the cool marble wall. Before she could register what was happening, he gathered her wrists and pinned them above her head with a single capable hand. And the last remaining traces of resistance melted away. She couldn't fight it anymore. Not from this position of delicious surrender. Her arms went lax, and somewhere in the back of her mind, a wall came tumbling down.

The breath rushed from her body, and a memory came into focus with perfect, crystalline clarity.

Let's make a deal. If neither of us is married by the time we turn thirty, we'll marry each other. Agreed?

Agreed?

Her eyes flew open.

"Allegra?" Zander loosened his hold on her wrists, and she grabbed onto his shoulders to keep from slumping to the ground.

She gazed up at him, wide-eyed. *My God, he was right about the promise. He's been right all along.*

She wasn't sure what brought it back. Maybe this room, where they'd spent so much time together. Maybe the kiss. It had been no accident this time. This was a kiss steeped with intention, as was Zander's loaded stare. His hands were planted against the wall on either side of her head, and he was all but searing her with his gaze.

Willing her to remember.

"It was here, wasn't it?" she whispered, pressing her fingertips to her lips. She was coming apart at the seams. How could she have forgotten? How?

It had been late one afternoon in September. Indian summer. Outside, steam rose from the streets, shimmering over the city in a sultry haze. Allegra was still dressed for dance class in a plain black leotard that stuck to her dewy skin like glue as she and Zander moved uptown. They'd practiced for hours that day, preparing for an upcoming competition. Afterward, they'd shared a plate of cheese fries at the diner and walked to the subway with their hands linked together like they sometimes did.

Touching Zander was second nature to Allegra back then. They spent so many hours in a dance hold that she almost felt incomplete on her own. Untethered. She'd never examined what that out of sorts feeling meant, because again, it was *Zander*. Her partner. Why shouldn't she feel safe and natural in his arms? Why shouldn't his hand fit so perfectly into the small of her back?

Their intimacy had been so casual that she'd thought

it was meaningless. She'd gotten it wrong. It wasn't meaningless. Quite the opposite.

She could practically hear his voice again, just as it had been that September day.

Let's make a deal. If neither of us is married by the time we turn thirty, we'll marry each other. Agreed?

He'd pulled her close, rested his forehead against hers and whispered those words to her fourteen years ago in this very spot. And something wild and strange had wound its way through Allegra. Something that had made her feel more connected to him than she'd ever been before.

There'd been no hesitation in her response.

Agreed.

Six days later, her family had perished.

Died on impact. Those had been the words the policeman used. *They never saw it coming.* As if that was a comfort, a balm.

Allegra had never seen it coming either. She wished she had. If this was her destiny, if this was the twisted hand she'd been dealt, why couldn't there have been a sign? Some kind of a warning? Even a hint?

What would she have done differently if she'd known?

Everything. Mainly, she wouldn't have insisted her mom and dad come see her dance.

This is my fault. The thought had lodged itself in her head, pushing everything else out. Everything pure and true and good. All the new feelings she'd begun to have about Zander were replaced with the horrible reality that she'd become an orphan in the blink of an eye.

But how could she have forgotten the promise they'd made to one another that day?

Because it hurt too much to remember.

She'd chosen to forget so she wouldn't have to think about what she'd left behind.

"Is there something you want to tell me, Allegra?" Zander pressed his forehead against hers and slid his hands down her arms until they stood hand in hand. Just like before.

"I remember our promise," Allegra whispered. She shook her head, vaguely aware that her face was wet with tears. When had she started to cry? "I'd forgotten. But now..."

Now she knew.

He squeezed her hands so hard they went numb. "Oh, sweetheart."

He bent to kiss her again. Allegra tipped her face upward, toward his. Hungry. Eager. Ready to kiss him with eyes wide-open. At last.

But something stopped him—a noise, the clearing of a throat. Zander froze with his face just a fraction of an inch away from hers.

"Why, Mr. Wilde. Is that you?"

Why now?

Zander closed his eyes and cursed under his breath. He needed to get himself together before he turned around to face the woman behind him. He'd been waiting the entire week to talk to her, but suddenly she was the last person he wanted to see.

He opened his eyes, and by some miracle, Allegra was still standing there, looking at him with eyes brimming with tears and memories. He couldn't have conjured a better kiss in his dreams. She *remembered.*

But for some twisted reason, fate had chosen this very moment to toss the Vows reporter in his path.

"I'm sorry," he whispered and reached to brush a tear from Allegra's face. "Just give me a minute."

She nodded, but Zander could see hesitation slipping back into her sapphire eyes.

Damn it. Why now?

He turned, straightened the knot in his tie and extended his hand. "Zander Wilde. Apologies, you've caught me in a private moment. And you are?"

He knew exactly who she was, of course. She was the spitting image of the photo in her byline. Even before he'd seen her, he'd known who she was simply by the tone of her voice. Inquisitive with an edge.

"Celestia Lane, from the *New York Times*." She gave his hand a firm shake. "So sorry to interrupt. Although you seem to have chosen an awfully public place for a private moment."

Zander gave her a tight smile. If she'd been anyone else, he would have told her in no uncertain terms to mind her own damn business. But he was keenly aware that the fate of his hotel rested in her hands.

"My mistake." He pasted a smile on his face. "It's a pleasure to finally meet you in person."

Celestia Lane nodded. Her gaze flicked over Zander's shoulder, toward Allegra.

Zander felt like he was watching the beginning of a terrible accident playing out in slow motion with his hands tied. "I apologize for missing our dinner meeting a few nights ago. An emergency situation came up, and I was unable to get a call through to the hotel."

"I see," Celestia said absently.

The columnist was hardly paying attention to what

he was saying. She seemed much more interested in Allegra. "Aren't you going to introduce me to your friend, Mr. Wilde?"

Zander hesitated.

Behind him, Allegra blurted, "I was just leaving."

No.

He turned and muttered, "Wait. *Please.*"

But she was already walking past him, headed for the door.

Celestia called after her. "Excuse me, do we know each other? You look familiar."

Zander cursed under his breath. The only way for this situation to get any worse would be if the reporter recognized Allegra as one of the Bennington's runaway brides. Specifically, Spencer Warren's runaway bride, the most notorious one of them all according to the Vows article.

The headlines would be devastating. The reporter would probably find a way to insinuate that Allegra's failed nuptials had something to do with her relationship with Zander. There was no doubt in his mind she'd exploit it. She'd turn whatever was going on between them into something ugly before the two of them even had a chance to figure it out for themselves.

It made Zander sick. Even so, he could understand it. Celestia Lane was a journalist, and he'd just been seen kissing one of the runaway brides a mere week after she'd fled her wedding ceremony at his cursed hotel.

It looked bad.

Very bad.

Allegra realized as much, too, obviously. She bowed her head and kept walking toward the exit. "Sorry, but you must be mistaking me for someone else. I don't live here. I'm just visiting."

She gave them both a quick wave, then pushed through the double doors, onto the snowy New York streets.

Just visiting. Zander told himself not to take those words to heart. Allegra hadn't necessarily meant them. She was trying to throw the reporter off the scent. But they seemed to lodge in his chest, choking him, all the same.

The reporter arched an eyebrow at Zander. "Your mystery woman forgot her coat."

He took a deep, pained breath. Things were getting worse by the minute. "I should go fetch it for her then. If you'll excuse me..."

"Of course." The reporter nodded. "It was a pleasure running into you, Mr. Wilde."

She turned to go, but not before shooting him an overly solicitous smile. A dreadful certainty settled over Zander.

He hadn't heard the last of Celestia Lane.

Chapter Twelve

Allegra sat at the kitchen table in the brownstone the next morning, staring at her cell phone.

The little black kitten was curled into a cuddly ball in her lap, and a lacy veil of frost covered the kitchen windows. Steam rose from the coffee cup situated on the place mat in front of her. Everything was so serene. So *homey.* Allegra wasn't sure she could go through with what needed to be done.

Just do it. Make the call.

She picked up the phone and scrolled through her contacts, searching for Talia's number with a shaky hand.

You're doing the right thing.

She absolutely was. Last night had been a wake-up call.

If the reporter from the Vows column hadn't interrupted them, there was no telling what would have happened. Allegra had been on the verge of sleeping with Zander, all because of a dreamy memory.

She'd tried to tell herself that nothing really happened, that it was just a kiss. But deep down, she knew better. Remembering the promise they'd made to one another had rocked her to her core. It plunged her right back into her past, made it seem like she was experiencing that day in the museum for the very first time. For a bittersweet moment, she'd almost believed she was sixteen again.

Well, she wasn't.

She was a grown woman, not a naive teenager. She couldn't go around kissing Zander anymore, acting as if they could turn back the clock. Promises had consequences. Belonging to someone meant losing them one day. She knew that now. And the pain of those consequences was more than she could bear.

"Allegra!" Talia answered on the first ring. Her voice was so animated that she sounded as though she'd been sitting by the phone, waiting for Allegra's call. "It's so great to hear from you. I was beginning to think you'd decided to stay in New York forever."

"No." Allegra swallowed around the lump in her throat.

Why was this so difficult?

She couldn't stay here. She couldn't keep working at the Wilde School of Dance, and she couldn't keep playing house with Zander, or whatever it was they were doing.

What *were* they doing, anyway?

"So does this call mean what I think it means?" Talia asked.

"That depends." Allegra took a fortifying sip of her coffee. "Is the corps de ballet spot on the touring company still available?"

Talia let out an earsplitting squeal, which Allegra took as a definitive *yes*.

"I knew you'd change your mind," she said. "Traveling the world…dancing in another city every night. What could be better?"

She was right. It sounded perfect. It was everything Allegra wanted.

Is it?

Zander strolled into the kitchen and smiled at her as he headed toward the coffeepot.

Allegra's heart gave a little lurch. "Right. I have some things to finish up here before I go, though. What day does the tour start again?"

She couldn't leave until after the dance marathon. She'd given Emily her word. She had to see it through. She *wanted* to. Too much, if she was being honest with herself.

Which was precisely why she needed to leave. Now, while she still could. She was becoming too comfortable here.

Too happy.

"We leave in two weeks. If you're serious about this you need to give the ballet director a call. Do you still have his contact information?"

"I do." Allegra did her best to ignore the hard stare Zander was now aiming her way from the other side of the room.

"Good. You need to call him right now. I'm not joking. Hang up and call him before it's too late. Promise me," Talia said.

"I promise." Allegra's gaze was glued to the table, but it made no difference. She could *feel* Zander's eyes on her.

This wasn't the way she wanted him to find out about the tour. She'd planned on telling him later, once it was official. She'd purposely gotten up while it was still dark outside so she could make the call before he was up and about.

Maybe it was better this way, though, like ripping off a Band-Aid. There was no sense in postponing the inevitable.

"Okay, I'm hanging up now so you can do it. Make the call. See you soon!"

The line went dead.

Allegra quietly set her phone back down on her place mat.

"Going somewhere?" Zander's voice was so sharp it could have cut glass.

Allegra lifted her chin. "Maybe." *Seriously?* That wasn't the way to rip off a Band-Aid. She took a deep breath. "I mean, yes. One of the dancers on the Boston Ballet's touring company is injured. The ballet director wants me to take her place."

"Congratulations are in order, then." A vein throbbed in his temple. "Were you going to mention it this time? Or were you planning on letting me wake up one day to find you gone?"

He looked furious. He also looked insanely handsome, with his hair slicked neatly back, dressed in another of his immaculate suits. The way he was glaring at her made it seem more like a three-piece suit of armor.

Not that she could blame him for being angry.

But honestly, did he have to be such a jerk about it? He couldn't *pretend* to be happy for her? "That's not fair, Zander. I was absolutely going to tell you. And I'm not going anywhere until after the dance marathon. I was actually hoping I could come by the Bennington today after I teach class so we could get going on the plans."

"Ryan can help you with the arrangements. I'll speak to him about it this morning." He crossed his arms and leaned back against the counter, his languid posture wholly at odds with the serious glimmer in his dark eyes. "When were you going to tell me?"

She should have known he wouldn't let it go.

Allegra swallowed. "Once it was certain. I haven't spoken to the ballet director yet. He may not even cast me."

Could she do this? Could she really walk away?

The kitten hopped down from her lap and padded toward Zander. She let out a mournful meow, rubbed her face against his shin and wound through his legs in a figure eight.

Allegra averted her gaze. "I'm not running away. This isn't like last time, Zander. I promise it's not."

"Really?" He bent to scoop the kitten into his arms. "Tell me how it's different."

"I didn't have a choice. You know that. My aunt was my legal guardian, and she lived in Cambridge."

"I'm aware. That's not what I'm talking about. I'm asking you why I never heard from you again after you left." His voice lowered an octave, and the rawness of it made it impossible for Allegra to look at him.

She closed her eyes. "We were kids. I'd just lost everything..."

I couldn't lose you, too.

But she had. She'd pushed him away, and here she was doing it again.

She opened her eyes and lifted her gaze to his. He was stroking the cat and his expression had softened a bit, but his eyes remained blank and unreadable.

Last night, the tenderness in his gaze had nearly brought her to her knees. For a brief, shining moment, her life had felt like one unbroken story, instead of what it really was—two pieces, sliced right down the middle, both of them incomplete.

"We were in love," he said woodenly. "I was, anyway."

Allegra opened her mouth to argue but closed it again.

He'd been in love with her? He'd never told her. She'd never said anything to him about how she felt either, but that didn't mean those feelings hadn't been there. Allegra couldn't pretend otherwise anymore. The kiss had brought everything back.

She inhaled a ragged breath. *No air. There is no air in this room.* "Well, we're not in love anymore. That's how it's different."

A strained, suffocating silence fell over the kitchen.

When Zander finally spoke, his seemingly random question caught Allegra by surprise. "Have you given this cat a name yet?"

The kitten was purring louder than a freight train in his arms. Allegra could hear it from clear across the room.

She shifted in her chair. "No, I haven't."

He shook his head. "I didn't think so."

Seriously? He'd gone from blatantly stating that he used to be in love with her to complaining about her pet-parenting skills? The man was impossible. “Why does it bother you so much that I haven’t named my kitten?”

“I thought she wasn’t yours.”

Allegra’s face went hot. “She’s not.”

He shrugged. “I suppose that’s a good thing since you can’t drag a cat around on a ballet tour.”

“Exactly.” Allegra hadn’t really thought about that yet, but it was fine. She truly had no intention of keeping the animal.

She glanced at the black kitten, looking tinier than ever slung over Zander’s impressive forearm. Again, the room seemed devoid of air.

She pressed a hand to her stomach, but before she could invent a reason to excuse herself, her cell phone blared to life on the kitchen table.

Allegra picked it up and glanced at the screen. “It’s the ballet director.”

Talia must have been so excited that she’d made the call herself.

“What are you waiting for? Answer it.” Zander pushed himself off the counter and deposited the kitten in Allegra’s lap. The cat stretched her tiny little legs and kneaded her paws on Allegra’s bathrobe.

Everything about this felt wrong. What was she doing? “Zander, I…”

But when Allegra looked up, the door was already clicking shut behind Zander’s back.

The morning meeting at the Bennington finished in record time. Not, however, because the night manager and the reservations supervisor didn’t have anything to report to Zander and Ryan. There was plenty to cover, including a rather sordid story about an award-winning actor who'd recently checked out after a full week in one of the penthouse suites. The meeting wrapped up early because Zander was operating like a machine.

A well-oiled one at that.

It felt good to throw himself back into his work. Work was logical. Sensible. The analytical nature of Zander's job was what attracted him to the business world over a decade ago. His acumen for facts and figures and his commanding presence were what kept him ensconced in the Bennington's corner office.

That commanding presence had been on full display since he'd taken a seat at the head of the conference room table at just after 8:00 a.m.

"I think we're finished here," he said, closing the leather portfolio embossed with the Bennington crest.

The people seated around the table glanced at one another and then filed quietly out of the room, with the exception of Ryan.

"Are you ready to go over the latest budget figures?" Zander motioned toward the spreadsheets fanned out in front of Ryan with his Montblanc fountain pen.

"Yes." Ryan gave him a slow nod, but made no move to reach for the documents. "Perhaps you want to talk about it first?"

Zander leaned back in his chair and crossed his arms. "Talk about what?"

"Whatever it is that's got you so wound up. You seem a little..."

Zander lifted an eyebrow. "Focused?"

Ryan nodded. "Staunchly so, yes."

"That's not a bad thing," Zander countered. "In fact, it's my job to stay focused on the Bennington."

Ryan held up his hands in a gesture of surrender. "No one's complaining. I just get the feeling there might be something you need to get off your chest."

"There isn't." Zander shook his head and dropped his gaze to the glossy surface of the conference room table.

What was there to talk about? Allegra was leaving. Discussing it with Ryan wouldn't erase the shock of walking into the kitchen earlier and overhearing her plans to go on an extended ballet tour. It wouldn't rid him of the heaviness he felt in his chest every time he thought about it.

It wouldn't make her stay.

"Okay, then." Ryan slid a copy of the hotel's latest profit-and-loss statement toward Zander.

"Wait, actually there's something I need to tell you." Zander leaned forward.

"Shoot."

He cleared his throat. "Allegra is putting together a fund-raiser for the Wilde School of Dance—a retro dance marathon. I told her she could have it here, in the ballroom. I'm assuming we still have availabilities next week?"

"We're wide-open." Ryan's gaze flitted to the column of red numbers on the financial statement. "Unfortunately."

"Good." Zander frowned. "Or not. You know what I mean. Anyway, I told Allegra you'd run point on this."

Ryan went silent for a beat. Then he said, "Really? I don't mind, but are you sure you don't want to handle it?"

"More than sure." Zander clenched his teeth.

He was as angry with himself as he was with Allegra. More so, actually.

Her news shouldn't have surprised him. He knew it was coming. Allegra ran. It's what she did.

When she was scared, she left and never looked back. If he'd thought for one moment the ballet tour was a career choice, he'd have been thrilled for her. Hell, he would have helped her pack her bags if it was what she really wanted.

But it wasn't. Her decision wasn't part of a career plan. She'd said herself that she wasn't a ballerina anymore. She was happy teaching at the studio. His mom couldn't stop talking about how much Allegra loved her students. She was a natural. He'd seen her teaching class, and she seemed happy. Happier than he'd seen her since before her family's accident.

He knew what was going on. Allegra was leaving because they'd shared a moment last night at the museum. She'd felt something for him. Something more than just desire.

And it scared the life out of her.

Ryan's gaze narrowed. He shrugged. "Fine. I just thought you might want to head this up since a dance marathon fits in with the retro-musical vibe you've been working so hard to establish here."

He was right. An event like the one Allegra had in mind perfectly matched the nostalgic ambience Zander aimed to achieve at the Bennington with the monthly Big Band Nights and the jazz bar he'd recently opened in the hotel lobby. To the staff they were known as Zander's passion projects.

"Plus you and Allegra have always made a good team," Ryan said quietly.

Zander let out a long exhale. "Years ago. Things change."

Then again, some things never did. History was repeating itself. Only this time, he and Allegra weren't kids. She had a choice this time. She could stay.

Stay.

Just four letters. One little word. Yet he'd been unable to make himself utter it earlier. He'd talked circles around it, but he'd never come out and asked her to stay.

What was the point? She'd been planning her escape since she'd moved into the brownstone. Who was he kidding, anyway? The only reason she was even in New York was because she'd nearly gotten married. It wasn't fate. It was just a big, messy mistake.

"So." He sighed. "You'll work with her on the dance marathon?"

"Sure." Ryan nodded, but he still looked doubtful.

Too bad. Zander wasn't changing his mind. "Great. Give her whatever she needs—catering, music. I'll leave it to your discretion. It's for the dance school, which could use the help, especially since the ballroom is sitting there empty, anyway."

Zander's executive assistant suddenly appeared in the doorway of the conference room. "Excuse me, gentlemen. There's someone here to see Mr. Wilde—a Ms. Celestia Lane from the *New York Times*."

Zander and Ryan exchanged a glance.

"Show her in," Zander said.

"Very well."

With the assistant out of earshot, Ryan muttered, "This should be interesting. I'm guessing there's something else you should probably fill me in on?"

"I ran into her last night."

What was she doing here? Zander had allowed himself to breathe a sigh of relief when there'd been no mention of the curse in the paper this morning. The Bennington had even managed to book a wedding. Just one…a month from now. But it was better than nothing.

Somehow, though, Zander had a feeling this impromptu visit from the Vows columnist wasn't good news.

"And?" Ryan asked under his breath.

Zander stood to button his suit jacket. "And I have no idea what she's doing here."

Ryan rolled his eyes. "Well, that explains everything."

Zander's assistant escorted the reporter into the room. Celestia declined her offer of sparkling water or a cappuccino and then smiled brightly at Zander. "Good morning, Mr. Wilde."

He knew right away something was off. She looked far too pleased with herself. "Good morning. This is a surprise."

He introduced her to Ryan and all three took a seat.

"What can I do for you, Ms. Lane?"

"You can give me a quote for my column tomorrow, for starters. It's all about how I saw the CEO of the Bennington in a 'private moment' with one of his hotel's runaway brides." She smirked. "At a wedding, no less."

Zander said nothing. Beside him, Ryan sighed and pinched the bridge of his nose.

"I knew your companion looked familiar. Imagine my surprise when I did a little digging and discovered she was none other than Allegra Clark, Spencer Warren's former fiancée." Celestia reached into her massive designer handbag and pulled out a notebook.

Zander looked pointedly at the notebook and rolled his eyes. "Save it. You didn't come here for a quote. If you were going to run with this story, you would have already done so."

Ryan cleared his throat. "Zander, maybe we should hear her out."

He lifted his eyebrows and waited for her to elaborate.

"The story will run in Vows tomorrow morning, with or without your input." She tapped her pen on her notepad and waited.

Zander still wasn't buying it. She wanted something, and that something wasn't a quote. She was holding out. He just wished he knew what for.

"You write for the *New York Times*, Ms. Lane. This kind of story is beneath both you and your publication. It's a gossip piece." He gave her a tight smile. "As is your curse theory."

"I agree." She shrugged. "Unfortunately, the curse story got a lot of traction. It's been very popular."

"I gathered." His empty ballroom spoke volumes.

"The readers want a follow-up story, and my editor is demanding that I give them one. Believe me, I'd rather write about a wedding here at the Bennington. But there don't seem to be many of those taking place." She sighed. "So why don't you tell me what I'm supposed to write about, Mr. Wilde?"

Zander should have been relieved. The ball was in his court.

But he couldn't come up with a single thing she'd be interested in.

Concentrate. There had to be something.

"I have an idea," Ryan said.

"Yes?" Celestia held her pen at the ready.

"Let's hear it," Zander said.

"Leave Zander and Allegra out of the paper, and in exchange we give you exclusive coverage of the next wedding to take place at the Bennington." Ryan smoothed down his tie. "You said you'd rather cover a wedding, so let's do it. The next time someone ties the knot here, we'll give you a front-row seat. If the bride runs, you'll have a story. If everything goes off without a hitch, you'll have one, too. It will be the end of the supposed curse. Either way, it's win-win."

Ryan's gaze flicked briefly toward Zander. Zander gave him a barely perceptible nod.

It was great idea. Fantastic, in fact.

Celestia smiled. "I like it."

"I thought you might," Ryan said.

"But I'd need a guaranteed invitation for both myself and my photographer."

Zander's answer was swift and unequivocal. "Done."

"Assuming we can get the bride and groom to agree, of course," Ryan added.

"They will." Celestia flipped her notepad closed. "Trust me, there isn't a bride on earth who doesn't want her wedding in the *Times*."

"So we have an agreement?" Zander stood and extended a hand.

"It looks like we do, Mr. Wilde." The reporter slipped her hand into his and gave it a shake.

Zander's mouth curved into a tight smile. "I look forward to not seeing my name in the paper tomorrow." *Or ever.*

"I'll be waiting for your call. Get in touch the minute you've got a date for me. I'll be here with bells on."

Celestia gave them both a flippy little wave on her way out. “Good day, gentlemen.”

Once she was gone, Zander’s smile faded. He shoved his hands into his trouser pockets and turned toward Ryan. “Why do I feel like we just made a deal with the devil?”

“Because we sort of did.”

Zander clenched his gut. “Not helping.”

“Don’t worry, cousin. We can use this to our advantage. Think about it—the guaranteed *Times* coverage is perfect. She’s right. Every couple in the city wants their wedding photo in her column. Give it a week. We’ll have more weddings booked here than we can handle.” Ryan cut him a triumphant grin.

He was right. The plan was brilliant. Unless…

“There’s just one hitch,” Zander said.

“I know.” Ryan nodded. “You don’t even have to say it.”

What if the bride runs?

Chapter Thirteen

Allegra stood beneath the glittering disco ball suspended from the ceiling of the Bennington Hotel's ballroom, not quite believing her eyes. "Ryan, how did you do this in less than ten days?"

The space had been transformed from top to bottom. If Allegra hadn't known better, she would have thought she'd stepped back in time. Red, white and blue bunting lined the walls, and streamers crisscrossed overhead. There were so many of them that she could barely see the deep blue ceiling, painted to look like a starry midnight sky. A bandstand was set up at the far end of the ballroom, and the parquet dance floor had been extended so it took up nearly the entire room. Allegra's favorite part of the entire setup, the pièce de résistance, was a wooden flip board with a vintage school clock for counting down the hours danced and the number of couples remaining in the marathon.

Everything was exactly as she'd envisioned it. Perfect. She felt as if she was standing inside a 1940s dance hall…

Or in the photograph of Zander's grandparents.

"Are you kidding? I didn't do all of this," Ryan said as he unfolded a white wooden folding chair to add to the section set up for spectators. "The staff helped. It's for a great cause. Everyone around here loves Emily and supports the school. They've all pitched in. It's been a group effort."

His gaze shot upward. "And as I recall, you were the one on a ladder at two in the morning hanging those streamers."

"Oh." She grinned. "I guess I was, wasn't I?"

"Yes, you were. If you forgot, it's probably because you've devoted so much time and energy to this dance marathon that you're delirious." Ryan plunked another chair into position. "I think we're ready, though. You should probably head to the brownstone and get some rest or you'll never manage to dance for twelve straight hours tonight."

Allegra's smile faded. "Oh, um, I'm headed out to change clothes and get ready, but I'm not dancing tonight."

Ryan planted his hands on his hips and frowned. "Is that a joke? You're not participating in this shindig? I figured you'd be the first one out on the dance floor cutting a rug."

Allegra rolled her eyes. "Cutting a rug? I think you're taking this whole retro thing a bit too seriously."

Ryan narrowed his gaze. "I see what's going on here. You're just like him, you know."

"Just like who?" Allegra busied herself securing

the corner of bunting so she wouldn't have to look him in the eye.

She had a good idea who he meant.

"Zander," Ryan said.

Bingo.

"I don't know what you're talking about. Zander and I—"

"Are both experts at deflection." He shook his head. "I've never seen two people so adept at changing the subject the minute the conversation becomes uncomfortable."

"I'm not uncomfortable." But the room suddenly felt very warm. "I'm just not planning on dancing tonight. I'll be far too busy."

"Which is exactly what Zander said earlier. Word for word." Ryan winked. "I rest my case."

Don't say anything. Do. Not.

"So Zander isn't planning on coming tonight?" Allegra said, because apparently no amount of self-lecturing could keep her mouth shut.

She couldn't help it. She had to ask.

Zander had clearly been avoiding her, and she'd been doing the same as far as he was concerned. They hadn't exchanged a word since the morning he'd walked in on her conversation with Talia. She'd barely set eyes on him, save for a glimpse of him every so often at the Bennington. Every time she spied him striding across the hotel's opulent lobby in one of his power suits, looking like he'd walked right off the cover of *GQ*, she turned and headed in the opposite direction.

But he was everywhere. The bridal curse no longer seemed to be hurting business. Zander had been parading brides-to-be around the hotel on a regular basis.

She wasn't sure how many weddings were actually on the books—if there were any—and she hadn't asked.

She didn't know what to say to Zander. He thought she was running away, and she wasn't sure how to convince him otherwise. Probably because a very small part of herself wondered if he might be right.

Ryan shrugged. "He hasn't said whether or not he'll show tonight, but he made it very clear he wouldn't dance."

"Well, that makes two of us." She couldn't. No way.

Dancing with Zander again would feel like ripping open an old wound. Or walking headlong into a memory—a memory that would leave her raw and vulnerable.

She couldn't be that close to him. She couldn't look him in the eyes while he held her, knowing he could feel the pounding of her heartbeat against his chest. Maintaining any sort of distance was hard enough when they were living under the same roof. It was impossible when he touched her.

The last time he'd been within a foot of her, she'd kissed him. Who knew what would happen if they danced together again?

At the same time, she couldn't fathom dancing with anyone else.

Zander was her first dance partner.

Her *only* dance partner.

There'd been a tenderness to their partnership that Allegra had never felt with another man. As ridiculous as it seemed, dancing with someone else would have felt like a betrayal.

Ryan shot her a weary glance. "Please tell me there are couples who've signed up for this event—couples who are planning on actually dancing instead of standing around pretending not to have feelings for each other."

"Plenty of people have registered for the marathon. Over one hundred couples, in fact." Allegra had uploaded notices on every dance-related group on social media that she could find. Plus the Bennington and the Wilde School of Dance both sent out email blasts. The event had already raised thousands, just in registration fees.

"That's fantastic," Ryan said. "I'm impressed."

"But you're wrong about Zander and me. We don't have feelings for each other." Allegra crossed her arms and then promptly uncrossed them. She couldn't seem to figure out what to do with them. Or where to look, because Ryan's gaze had quickly become too probing. Too *knowing.*

"Are you sure about that?"

"Absolutely," she said.

Liar.

She bit the inside of her mouth.

Her bags were packed. Her plane ticket was booked. There was no reason to stick around after the dance marathon. She was flying to Boston in the morning, just in time to join the company tour. This time next week, she'd be onstage. A different city every day.

"As long as you're sure," Ryan said.

He didn't finish the thought. He didn't have to.

As long as you're sure, because after tomorrow it will be too late.

"Everything is in order for your wedding next weekend." Zander turned to face the couple he was escorting from his office to the Bennington entrance. He smiled.

"You have my personal assurance that the ceremony will proceed perfectly according to plan."

Unless you dash out of the building in a puff of lace and tulle. He glanced at the bride and somehow managed to bite his tongue.

"Excellent." The groom-to-be shook Zander's hand.

He held the door open for them, and the happy couple exchanged a giddy glance before heading out into the bitter New York air.

Zander had witnessed a lot of those giddy glances over the past week. He'd been working overtime to get a wedding booked as soon as possible. Fortunately, Ryan's outrageous idea seemed to be working.

Curse or no curse, guaranteed coverage in the Vows column was too tempting for most Manhattan brides to resist. The phones at the Bennington were ringing again. Zander was neck-deep in lovey-dovey couples. He should have been used to the wistful glances by now, but somehow witnessing them always felt like getting punched in the gut.

He took a seat on one of the plush velvet sofas in the hotel lobby, scrolled through the contacts on his cell phone and stopped when he reached the entry for the Vows desk.

Celestia answered on the first ring. "Hello, Mr. Wilde."

"Ms. Lane." Zander did his best to sound polite. It was a stretch after everything the reporter had put him through. "I'm calling to let you know we've got a wedding confirmed for later this week."

He gave her the necessary details.

"Perfect. My photographer and I will both be there." She sounded positively elated, which only exacerbated Zander's dark mood.

You'd better be there. "Good. And nothing new in the paper before then, correct?"

"That was our deal, and I'm standing by it," she said.

How had he managed to let the fate of his hotel rest in this horrible woman's hands?

"But you've got to hold up your end, as well. If another wedding takes place before then, I expect a call."

"Understood," Zander said.

He ended the call as quickly as possible.

It was almost over—the curse business, Allegra, all of it.

Everything was falling into place nicely. At last. He should have been happy. Hell, he should have been doing cartwheels down one of the Bennington's hallways.

A man and woman stumbled past him from the direction of the ballroom. They were both flushed and slightly disheveled, hanging on to one another for support. But their wide smiles radiated joy, and one of them was humming a tune—"Walkin' My Baby Back Home."

Zander looked away.

He'd managed to avoid the dance marathon thus far. It had started hours ago, and the air in the Bennington had been thick with music all evening. Big-band standards like "In the Mood" and "Sing, Sing, Sing (With a Swing)."

Zander was determined to stay away. Doing so had been relatively easy—or possible, at least—while he'd been busy with bridal appointments. But now his foot was tapping along to the faint strains of an old Frank Sinatra tune.

He stood, fully intent on summoning his driver and

heading back to the brownstone. But instead of walking toward the valet, he found himself drawn to the ballroom. He told himself he was simply doing the right thing, fulfilling his obligation as a Wilde. The event was a fund-raiser for his mother's school after all. How would it look if he didn't even make an appearance when the big dance was taking place right under his roof? The entire family would be there—Emily, Ryan, Tessa and Julian. Even Chloe had promised to show up, dragging one of the Rockettes' stagehands along as her dance partner.

Zander's absence would have been notable.

Five minutes.

That's it. He'd stay for one song—two max—and then get the hell out.

The music grew louder as he approached. Zander paused at the ballroom entrance, bracing himself, but he was swept into the jubilant crowd almost at once. The room was full to bursting. Couples spun past him, dancing the Charleston and the Lindy Hop and a few other dance variations he remembered from his brief tenure as a competitive dancer.

He backed out of the way as the couple right in front of him stopped in place to do a crocodile roll. The male dancer's legs parted, and his partner shot between them, flipped over, then popped back up into a dance hold.

The space was a hive of activity. He'd never seen anything like it, even on the occasions the Bennington had hosted Big Band Night. This was Big Band Night on steroids.

Despite the crowd and the noise and the wall-to-wall revelry, Zander's gaze immediately found Allegra, as though drawn to her by some invisible force. A feeling passed through him that felt too much like relief when he saw her walking toward the bandstand with her full skirt and red crinolines swishing around her slender legs. She was breathtaking, wearing a white halter-style dress decorated with bright red cherries and her hair swept away from her face in double victory rolls.

More important, she was alone.

The tension that had gathered between Zander's shoulder blades loosened a little. He wasn't sure what he would have done if he'd walked into the ballroom and seen Allegra dancing with someone else. He just knew that a part of him would have died inside.

He realized it wasn't rational. It definitely wasn't fair. This was a dance marathon, and he and Allegra weren't even technically speaking to one another at the moment. He had absolutely no right to expect her to stay off the dance floor.

He didn't care, though. He was past the point of pretending anything he felt for Allegra made sense. And he definitely felt…something.

He couldn't identify what those feelings were, other than they were mired in history and laced with a vague sense of regret.

He shoved his hands into his pockets and leaned against the wall as he watched her climb the steps of the bandstand and position herself behind the microphone. He had no reason to regret anything. She'd made her choice, and there was nothing he could do about it.

"Impressed?"

Zander turned. His mother stood beside him, dressed in khaki with a military hat propped on top of her head at a jaunty angle.

"Love the outfit," he said. "It's very 'Boogie Woogie Bugle Boy.'"

"Thanks." She aimed a questioning glance at his tie. "Honestly, couldn't you have dressed for the occasion? You look like a corporate raider who wandered in here by mistake."

Zander's jaw clenched. "I look like a CEO, because that's what I am."

"Message received. You're not dancing tonight." She sighed and leaned closer so she wouldn't have to yell over the music. "But that doesn't mean I'm letting you off the hook. You still haven't answered my question. Impressed?"

He nodded. "Quite. This is really something. I'm guessing the school will be in a much better financial position after tonight."

"It will." His mother cleared her throat. "But that's not what I meant."

Her gaze cut to the bandstand, where Allegra was about to address the crowd. "She's remarkable, isn't she?"

"Yes." Zander sighed. "She's also leaving tomorrow."

"Right. But she's not gone yet, is she?" Emily winked at him.

"I think it's time for me to go." Zander pushed off the wall, but his mom snagged him by the elbow as Allegra's voice rang out over the loudspeaker.

"Congratulations, dancers! You've made it past the three-hour mark!" Her eyes met his across the crowded room. There was an unmistakable hitch in her voice, but she continued. "Don't forget to dance past the water station. In about half an hour, we'll have volunteers passing out sandwiches. In the meantime, dance on!"

The dancers all cheered, and the opening bars of Glenn Miller's "A String of Pearls" rang out as she stepped away from the podium.

Zander lost track of her in the crowd, but he knew she was making her way toward him. He could feel it.

Which was definitely his cue to leave, but he couldn't seem to make his feet budge.

"Zander! We've been wondering when you'd show up, right, Mom?" Tessa threw her arms around his neck and kissed his cheek. "Isn't this fantastic? I can't believe Allegra put this together so quickly." She waved an arm toward the dance floor.

Zander waited for Tessa to face him again before he responded so she could read his lips. "It's remarkable. But where's your dance partner?"

He signed the words in addition to speaking them. Tessa was almost completely deaf as a result of a head injury she'd suffered in dance class a few years ago. She hadn't let her physical challenges stand in her way, though. She'd since become one of the Manhattan Ballet's most popular principal dancers.

"Julian's playing piano with the band." She smiled at her fiancé, pounding away on a white baby grand in the center of the stage. "But that means I'm free if you want to take me for a spin. How about it? Do you want to dance?"

The moment the words left Tessa's mouth, Allegra reached the edge of their grouping. The timing couldn't have been more awkward, unless, of course, Allegra hadn't overheard anything.

But the stiff smile on her face told Zander she was fully aware what Tessa had just said. Their eyes met and held for a second, until she dropped her gaze to the floor.

Tessa turned to face her. "Allegra, look who finally decided to show up."

Allegra glanced at him again and swallowed. "Hello, Zander."

Tessa sighed. "I was just trying to persuade him to dance with me, but as you can see, he looks less than thrilled at the prospect."

"Tessa." Zander shot his sister a warning glance, but she was facing the opposite direction, still chattering away, oblivious.

Emily released her hold on Zander's elbow and touched Tessa gently on the shoulder, capturing her attention. "Can you come help me with something, dear?"

Tessa shrugged. "Sure." She extended her hands, palms facing up, and moved them back and forth in the ASL motion for *what?*

"Dance-school business," Emily said. She wrapped her arm around Tessa's waist and pulled her away.

Tessa shot a confused glance over her shoulder, then looked back and forth between Zander and Allegra. "Oh." Her eyes grew wide. "Of course. Happy to help."

Zander let his eyes drift shut and took a deep breath. He knew he should have stayed away.

When he opened his eyes, Allegra was still there. She'd moved to stand beside him, so they were facing the dance floor, side by side.

"You could have danced with your sister, you know. It wouldn't have bothered me," she said, refusing to meet his gaze. Her attention remained firmly fixed on the couples twirling across the room.

"Note taken." He suppressed a smile.

He didn't believe her for a minute, even though the potential dance partner in question was his sister. The situation couldn't have been more innocent.

That didn't matter, though. Zander understood. He would've felt jealous beyond all reason if he'd just seen someone else ask Allegra to dance, be it George Clooney or her great-grandfather.

He sneaked a glance at her profile. God, she was gorgeous. The surroundings, steeped in nostalgia, emphasized her timeless beauty. She never failed to take his breath away—yesterday, today, tomorrow.

A bottomless sense of loss settled in the pit of his stomach.

What if there is no tomorrow?

Every instinct he possessed told him to look away. Not just *look* away, but *walk* away, too. Walk away without a backward glance.

Instead he let his attention linger on the graceful curve of her neck and then drift to the lush swell of her lower lip, as red and tempting as ripe fruit.

A pair of dancers bumped into Zander from behind, waving an apology as they danced past. Zander's knuckles brushed against Allegra's. She still didn't look at him, but instead of pulling her arm away, her fingertips laced gently with his.

Zander grew very still as they stood hand in hand. Connected, yet at the same time, miles apart. The fact that he couldn't bring himself to let go, even though he knew what sadness dawn would bring, made him realize that this night, this sliver of a moment, was their second chance.

Their *last* chance.

He gave her hand a tender squeeze, and at last she turned her gaze on him. Her sapphire eyes were red rimmed, shiny and wet with a bittersweet combination of pain and hope. Shattered bits of sparkle.

He didn't want to remember her this way. If this was the image of Allegra he was left with, he'd never forgive himself.

He ran the pad of his thumb along the palm of her hand. "Shall we dance?"

She bit her lip, and for a prolonged moment, Zander forgot how to breathe. Then she smiled a smile that reached all the way to her eyes. "I thought you'd never ask."

Chapter Fourteen

Allegra allowed Zander to lead her onto the dance floor and pretended not to notice the stares of his family members.

But they were all watching from the other side of the room, making the moment seem even more significant than it already was. She even thought she saw Ryan do a double take when he looked up from his glass of champagne and spied them together beneath the glittering disco ball.

"Ignore them," Zander whispered, pulling her into his arms. "Pretend it's just you and me out here. Just like old times."

She let out a nervous laugh and forced herself to relax against his body. "Pretend. Got it."

She could do that. She'd been pretending for such a long time that she was practically an expert.

You wanted this, remember?

She did. She'd wanted to dance with Zander since the second he'd walked into the ballroom. Not doing so felt wrong on every possible level. In some corner of her mind, she still knew it was a very bad idea, but her body didn't seem to care. She belonged in his arms with her legs and feet moving in time with his.

But now that it was actually happening, she wondered if she could actually go through with it.

Had dancing with him always felt so…

Intimate?

There was no other word for it, really. His face was only a breath away. She could feel the steady pounding of his heart against her chest. And the skillful way he took the lead, guiding her movements, made her weak in the knees.

If this was what it felt like to dance with Zander Wilde, what would it feel like to go to bed with him?

Her gaze slid toward him, and she tried to imagine it, grateful that he couldn't read her mind.

"Is everything in order for your trip tomorrow?" he murmured.

She blinked. Were they really going to talk about her departure while they were dancing?

"Well?" He raised a single dark eyebrow.

Apparently so.

Maybe it was for the best. Maybe, just *maybe*, if they had this conversation now, she could convince herself that the dance was simply a dance. Nothing more. Just two people swaying to the music. Maybe she could even manage to ignore the shiver that coursed through her every time her hip brushed against Zander's groin. Maybe she could forget the gentle pressure of his hand on the small of her back, and the way the heat of his touch seemed to burn right through her dress.

"Yes." She swallowed. Who was she kidding? She wouldn't have been any less aware of Zander's touch if she'd been forced to solve a complex math equation. As it was, she could barely speak in anything but monosyllables. "Train."

The corner of his mouth hitched into a knowing smirk.

She took a deep breath. "I mean, the train. I'm taking it from Grand Central to Boston in the morning."

Barely coherent, but at least she'd managed to form a full sentence.

"I see." His fingertips dipped lower, grazing her bottom.

He seemed cool as a cucumber, wholly unaffected by the slide of her thigh between his legs as they crossed the dance floor. It was beyond irritating.

She lifted her chin and did her best to mirror his detachment. "Look, I know you're angry that I'm leaving. You may as well admit it."

"I'm not angry, Allegra," he said evenly.

Her heart gave a little hitch. Her stupid, stupid heart.

So he wasn't angry. He was just indifferent.

"Good." She stiffened a little, and he seemed to sense it.

He pulled her closer. "You seem disappointed. And here I thought the kind thing to do would be to let you go without any histrionics."

He was right. What was wrong with her? She didn't want to leave on bad terms. She just wanted to know that he felt *something*. It didn't have to be anything close to the deeply rooted feelings she had for him.

So now you have feelings for Zander Wilde?

She cleared her throat. Of course she didn't have feelings for him. She just couldn't think straight while her body was pressed so firmly against the solid wall of his chest and while his lips brushed against her ear every time he dipped his head to speak to her. It was utterly confusing. She'd never felt so irritated, sad and aroused all at the same time.

"I'm not disappointed," she countered.

"You really think I don't know you well enough to sense when you're upset? Think again." A telltale knot of muscle flashed in his jaw. Maybe he wasn't quite as disinterested as she'd thought.

"Aha. You *are* mad. I knew it." She grinned triumphantly.

"You're ridiculous." He shook his head, but the corner of his mouth hitched into a half grin.

"Is it really so ridiculous to want to get everything out in the open before I leave again?"

He paused, and his gaze darkened. "Everything?"

Now was the time to change the subject, to say something frivolous and go back to ignoring the swirl of maddening emotion that simmered just below the surface whenever they were in a room together.

But she couldn't. Not while they were dancing.

"Sure. All of it." Dread mingled with the delicious heat that had settled low in her belly. "What would you like to know?"

"Tell me why you never came back, why I never heard from you again." His eyes shifted away from her, and his grip on her hand seemed to involuntarily tighten. "I missed you like hell."

The breath rushed from her body, and she glanced toward the exit.

"Don't even think about running away from me, Allegra. You're the one who started this. Now we're going to finish it. Tell me." His fingertips pressed more firmly into her back until she was flush against him.

She could feel everything, every part of him. There was nothing between them but an unsettling intimacy that squeezed the air from her lungs. Even though it frightened her to death, she couldn't tell him anything other than the truth. "Because it hurt too much to be here, Zander."

His gaze shifted back to her, his expression unreadable. "Does it still?"

"Sometimes." She swallowed hard. "It's just easier to be away."

"Away?" He shook his head and his footsteps slowed, until they were almost standing still in the center of the dance floor while dozens of other couples twirled and spun around them. As if they were stuck, suspended in a moment, while time kept whirling on in dizzying *pirouettes*. "You mean it's easier to be *alone*."

Such raw, honest words. Words she couldn't bring herself to say. She couldn't even form a response.

"You can't even commit to a stray cat. That's no way to live, Allegra." He stared her down, daring her to argue. As if she was his opponent instead of his dance partner.

She looked at him standing there with his self-righteous expression, and she was suddenly enraged. Enraged for reasons too numerous to count, but mainly at his ability to see straight through her, even after all this time.

"You have a lot of nerve, you know." She glared at his broad shoulders and realized she was mad at them, too, for being so strong, so damn tempting. Solid and muscular, as if they could carry a world of burdens. "You're angry at me for leaving and never coming back. But you knew where I was the whole time. If I was so important to you, why didn't you ever come to Boston? It's just a train ride away."

Their feet slowed to a complete stop. Zander let go of her hand in order to cup her face and force her to meet his gaze. His eyes were darker than ever. Dark and serious. He was quiet for a long moment, and the silence between them was so thick it seemed to drown out the music coming from the bandstand.

Finally, he spoke. "Who says I didn't?"

Her heart slammed against her rib cage. "What?"

He couldn't have come to Boston. She would have known. It couldn't be true.

But the look on his face told her it was. His lips inched upward into a smile so weighed down by sadness that she could barely stand to look at it. Nor could she bring herself to look away.

"When?" she breathed.

"Opening night of *Giselle*. I went to see you dance. It was about a month after I called off my wedding."

None of the words coming out of his mouth were making sense. He'd been in the audience at the Boston Opera House?

Now that she thought about it, she realized that's how Emily must have known to invite her to teach at the Wilde School of Dance. But that didn't explain why Zander had come all the way to Boston and never said anything.

He'd come to find her right after calling off his *wedding.*

That had to mean something.

"I don't understand. Why didn't you tell me? Why didn't you let me know you were there?" She shook her head.

This was the moment of truth, and it never would have happened if they hadn't danced together. She'd known all along that dancing was the one thing that would break down the wall between them, and she'd been right. The wall hadn't just fallen. Zander had smashed it into a pile of rubble at their feet.

"I went to bring you roses backstage, but somebody beat me to it." His smile hardened into place.

Heat rushed to Allegra's face. "Spencer."

He nodded. "I saw him knock on your dressing-room door. When you opened it, I noticed the diamond solitaire on your finger and put two and two together."

She felt like crying all of a sudden. She'd spent so much of her life grieving, and now this loss felt like one too many. A missed chance.

"Why?" she said hoarsely.

"Because above all, I wanted you to be happy. You deserve that, Allegra. You deserve all the happiness in the world. At the time it looked like you'd found that with Spencer, so I came back to New York."

"No." She shook her head. "I mean why did you go to Boston in the first place? Why did you go there to find me after such a long time?"

He reached up, brushing his fingertips lightly against her cheek. Her throat tightened. Desperation clawed at her like an animal. This wasn't the same as hearing he'd loved her when they were teenagers.

He'd come to find her. She almost wanted to clamp her hands over her ears because she knew whatever he was about to say wouldn't be something she could push away and pretend didn't matter.

She wasn't ready to hear it.

But if not now, when?

"It's you, Allegra. It's always been you."

Air.

She needed air.

"Allegra?" Zander's brow creased, changing his tender expression to one of concern.

She nodded. "I'm…" *Fine. Totally fine.*

Except she wasn't. How could she possibly be, after what Zander had just said to her?

She swallowed. "Actually, can we go?"

"You want to leave?" He searched her gaze.

"I do." Heat rushed through her face. She glanced around at the other dancers, spinning like tops, then back up at Zander.

Bits of light reflected off the disco ball, showering him in radiant prisms. He looked as though stars had fallen from the sky and landed on his shoulders. She suddenly wanted to be alone with him. She wanted that very much, more than she could possibly articulate.

"Take me home? Please?" she asked, sliding her hands down his arms and weaving her fingers through his. Then she directed her gaze very purposefully at his mouth.

"Absolutely." His voice dropped deliciously low, and it scraped her insides, leaving her even more raw and vulnerable than she'd felt after his startling admission.

Their remaining moments at the Bennington passed

in a blur of cheery goodbyes and assurances from Ryan and Emily that she'd done more than enough. Of course they'd stay and see the marathon through until the end. The music seemed to be moving at double speed, and her head spun. She almost felt as if she was hovering above the scene, watching the girl with the cherries on her dress being escorted from the ballroom by the dashing Zander Wilde.

Then they were on the sidewalk, beneath the golden glow of the Bennington's marquee, where he kissed her. And she was right back in the moment, where everything was sharp and real. A shiver coursed through her, and Zander slung his coat over her shoulders while they waited for the car, but she wasn't cold at all. She was hot. Her veins were on fire, and she felt too much. Wanted too much.

She wanted *him*. Now.

They barely made it through the door of the brownstone before he pinned her against the kitchen counter and kissed her gently before catching her bottom lip in a tantalizing bite. She gasped, and his mouth dropped to her neck while his hands slid to her wrists, ringing them like bracelets as he held her in place.

Then he angled his head and kissed a trail from her jaw to her shoulder, and she thought she might die right then and there.

"I need to see you," he groaned against her sensitive skin.

She could feel the length of his erection pressing against her through their clothes like an erotic promise as she reached behind her neck to unfasten the closure of her halter dress. She held her breath as her dress fell away.

"So beautiful," he whispered, and she could feel his eyes on her as real as a caress.

He didn't touch her until she was completely exposed, with her dress and panties pooled at her feet. She was burning, desperate for his hands, his tongue, his manhood.

And there was no awkwardness, no hesitation whatsoever. It seemed like the most natural thing in the world to be bared to him, to sigh into him as he cupped her breasts and his mouth found her nipple.

"Zander." Her voice was a breathy plea.

The ache inside in her was nearly intolerable. Bottomless and deep, and somehow tied specifically to Zander. To the bond they shared. It was agonizing and exquisite, all at once.

He sucked hard at her nipple, then released it and blew gently on her puckered flesh.

"Zander, please…" she begged.

"Tell me." He sounded every bit as tortured as she felt. "Tell me what you want, darling."

"This." She reached to take hold of his hard length through his trousers, earning a low, masculine growl.

Her heart felt like it was going to pound right out of her chest as he scooped her into his arms and carried her through the darkened house, toward his bedroom.

What were they doing?

Was this a mistake?

It no longer mattered. There was no turning back. She'd made up her mind. Long ago, if she was really being honest. It felt like they'd been spiraling toward this moment since the second she'd burst in on his birthday party. She closed her eyes, and she could still see his stunned face, lit by his birthday candles.

Make a wish.

Maybe he had. She definitely wished for this at some point along the way. Now here they were, and as much as she wanted it, the reality of what they were about to do frightened the life out of her.

"This doesn't change anything," she whispered into the warm crook of his neck.

She was still leaving. This wasn't a promise. It was a goodbye. The only *proper* goodbye, the only way she'd ever be able to walk away.

She'd never be able to tell Zander what he meant to her. Her bruised and battered heart wouldn't let her. Even if she'd been capable of that kind of vulnerability, she'd never have been able to find the words.

How did you tell someone they were the family you always wanted, the home you'd never really had? What ceremony of words could impart that kind of bond? Did such words even exist?

If they did, Allegra didn't know them. Words would never be enough. Her body would tell him. When he touched her, there were no lies, no holding back. The truth was in the shiver that coursed through her when his mouth closed around her nipple again. It was in the heat gathering in her center as he set her gently on the bed and his fingers slipped inside her while his thumb circled her with a finesse that she'd never known.

A sob rose to the back of her throat, even as her hips strained upward, seeking relief. Seeking *him.*

She refused to cry. She didn't want tears. She wanted to know what it felt like to have Zander inside her. She tugged at his clothes, fisting her hands in the sleek silk of his suit jacket until he paused long enough to undress. Then he was on the bed beside her, all lean muscle and taut bronze skin. So big. So warm. So very, very, hard.

It's you, Allegra. It's always been you.

The tears were coming, whether she wanted them or not. She squeezed her eyes closed tight, fighting them as best she could.

"Open your eyes, baby." His lips touched hers, gently this time. Tender and sweet. But his mouth was hot and ripe with delicious promises. He was taking her somewhere she'd never been—to a place where there was no turning back. "Look at me."

He was poised at her entrance, waiting. Wanting.

She did as he said and opened her eyes.

This doesn't change anything.

But as he pushed inside her, filling her at last, she knew it was a lie. Change was inevitable. It was already happening. She was opening to him. Not just her body, but her heart. Her soul. Her everything.

They wouldn't be the same after tonight—neither of them. *Everything* would change. It already had.

"You're so beautiful." He cradled her face in his hands as he began to move, sliding in and out of her.

Somewhere beneath the swirl of heat and pleasure, Allegra realized it was like dancing. The connection was so similar, but far more intense. Two bodies moving together in perfect sync—the hypnotic push and pull, the fire in Zander's eyes as he guided her through the rhythm, setting a pace that kept her right on the edge of coming apart.

Dancing had always been what they'd done best together. No fumbling words, no fear of letting go—just the music and the fluidity of their footsteps and absolute trust in one another. It was like that now, too, only instead of music, they moved in time to the sound of their shuddering breaths, the sweetest of sounds.

It had never been like this for Allegra with anyone else. She knew it never would again. This was it. This was the way it was supposed to be, the way it was when two people were in love.

Her breath caught in her throat.

Love?

No. She wasn't in love. She couldn't be. She didn't *want* to be. Love led to pain—the kind of pain that dragged you to your knees. She'd been through that before, and it had taken her years to learn to stand upright again.

No. She swallowed hard and shook her head, but then Zander's hips began to roll in an excruciatingly slow, seductive circle and his hands slid to cup her bottom, holding her still as he ground into her. She gasped and arched against him, alive with sensation. "Yes, Zander. Yes."

A deep shuddering moan slipped from her lips as her hands traveled down the length of Zander's back. She wanted to touch him everywhere. She wanted her fingertips to memorize every square inch of his hard, muscled body—every dip and plane.

He made a growling sound she'd never heard from him before. It was the sound of infinite satisfaction. Purely male. Purely sublime. It was so raw, so intense, that it nearly did her in.

Was this the same man she'd known nearly all her life? This fierce, powerful lover?

He was. And on some level she'd known it would be like this. Deep down in her marrow, she'd known.

Because she knew Zander. She knew the real him, and he knew her like no one else ever had. Ever would.

That's why this giving herself to him mattered. She knew it did, even as she pretended to believe otherwise.

"Come with me, darling," he murmured into her hair.

She could feel his pleasure building in time with hers. Every muscle in his body was tense, and his signature control was slipping away with each thrust. He was right on the brink with her, dancing on the edge. Then his teeth scraped her collarbone, and she couldn't hold back any longer.

She shattered around him, climaxing hard. But she never broke her gaze. She watched him through it all, wanting, *needing*, to remember everything about this moment—the tremble that racked through him as he found his release, the tender way he held her through the aftershocks and, most of all, the look in his eyes.

She could see a world in those deep brown irises she knew so well. A shimmering, beautiful future. Her and Zander. A real family. A life—hers for the taking.

If only she could be brave enough to grab hold of it.

Within minutes of spilling himself inside Allegra, Zander was hard again. When he touched her, when he kissed her, everything seemed to come alive. He'd known it would be like this when they finally dropped all pretenses and gave themselves to one another.

Yet the intensity of their connection also took him by surprise. How could he have been prepared for the reality of Allegra's beautiful body? For the satisfaction he found in every little whimper she made when he pushed her thighs apart and licked her until she cried his name? If a lifetime of knowing her hadn't prepared him, nothing could have. She was a sensual surprise and the most constant object of his desire, both at once.

She arched against his mouth as he pushed a finger inside her. So warm. So wet. He paused to watch her, glorious in the darkness.

Slow down. His thoughts were screaming. *Make it last.*

But he couldn't. He could barely keep himself from coming again and she wasn't even touching him. He was scarcely in control of his desire, scarcely in control of anything. Time was slipping away…seconds were passing with each kiss, each undulation of her perfect hips.

One night wasn't enough. How was he supposed to discover all her secret wants, her most hidden yearnings, when he couldn't hold back his hunger for her? He'd been waiting so long, *wanting* so long, that he was like a man who suddenly found himself drowning after a decade without water.

Breathe. Just take a breath and savor.

But her hands were in his hair, tugging hard. And before he could stop himself, he was sliding up the length of her body and entering her again, shuddering at the feel of her velvet heat.

His mind went blank then. Her hands slid to his backside, forcing him deeper, and he gave himself up to pleasure. He pumped harder, faster, until, in a staggering moment of restraint, he stopped just long enough to flip their position so she sat astride him.

She'd never looked as beautiful as when she rode him, breasts swaying in the silver moonlight, her hair spilling down her back. *This*, he thought, *this right here.* This was the way he'd remember her after she left. With fire in her eyes, not tears. Fire and light. Light so bright it seemed to reach straight into his chest and set him aflame.

He felt it hours later, smoldering deep inside. His need for her was constant…there, always there…even as she fell asleep with her limbs draped languidly over his and her waves of hair fanned out on his pillow. Even as he closed his eyes and the night finally claimed him.

Even when he woke up to the soft rays of morning and found her gone.

Chapter Fifteen

Zander went through the motions of searching the brownstone for any sign of Allegra on the off chance that she'd simply sneaked out of bed for a glass of water or something.

But it wasn't necessary.

He knew.

She wasn't there. He knew because she'd somehow taken the air out of the brownstone with her. He walked from room to room with a knot in his chest, struggling to take a breath.

There wasn't a sign of her anywhere—not in the upstairs guest room where she'd slept for the past several weeks, not at the big farm table where she liked to dawdle over her morning coffee and most notably, not in his bed. If the pillow beside his hadn't been warm to the touch, he might've been afraid he'd imagined their fateful reunion and that she'd never actually come back to New York at all.

He lowered himself into one of the chairs at the kitchen table and dropped his head into his hands. How could he have been such a fool? He'd actually allowed himself to believe that making love to Allegra had meant something. Because that's what it had been—love. Not just sex.

He was in love with Allegra Clark.

And just like last time, she'd left without saying goodbye.

But not everything was the same as it was last time, was it? He'd been blindsided when she'd gone to live with her aunt in Cambridge without giving him a chance to tell her how he felt. This time, he'd known it was coming. He'd hated it, but he'd known.

She'd even reminded him of the truth of the matter last night. She'd been naked in his arms, bared and beautiful, but still she'd made her intentions clear.

This doesn't change anything.

He'd heard it, but he refused to believe it.

He lifted his head and stared at the empty chair across from him. Her presence was somehow still there, as if she'd left part of herself behind. A ghost, haunting him with reminders of what should have been.

He closed his eyes and saw himself going through the motions of everyday life—meetings at the hotel, family events, meaningless dates with women whose names he wouldn't bother committing to memory.

He could do these things.

He'd done them before.

After the trip he'd made to Boston to see Allegra dance *Giselle*, he'd reset the clock. He'd finally let go.

Had it hurt? Of course. Back then, he'd let himself believe that despite the fact that they hadn't set eyes on one another in over a decade, he could bring her back. Or he could stay there with her, if necessary. He'd have given up the Bennington. He'd have given up everything to repair the damage done all those years ago.

But the ring on her finger had been a wake-up call. The time had come to move on. For good.

And he had.

If he could do it once, he could do it again.

He stood and headed for the French press. This was how people started over—by doing one thing at a time. First, coffee. Then…

He didn't have a clue, but he'd figure it out.

On the way to the cabinet, his foot made contact with something hard and sent whatever it was skidding across the kitchen floor. He let out a string of curse words, but when he bent to inspect his throbbing toe, his gaze landed on the offending object.

It was the china saucer that Allegra had been using to feed her kitten. Correction: the kitten she adored but insisted didn't actually belong to her.

Zander picked it up and ran his thumb along the saucer's rim. It had a tiny nick on the edge, much like the mysterious notch he'd noticed on one of the little black cat's ears.

Something about that tiny chip caused him to come undone. He wasn't entirely sure why. Maybe because he'd stumbled upon a physical reminder that Allegra had actually been there. Or maybe it was because Allegra and the little cat had a few things in common.

Both wild. Both fragile. Both deserving of far more than the lousy hand life had dealt them.

As if on cue, the cat materialized. She leaped from a shadowy corner of the room and landed on Zander's shoulder. He reached up and gathered her in his arms, and a purr rumbled deep in her tiny chest.

"You're home," he murmured, running his thumb between the kitty's ears. "I think it's time to go find her and bring her home, too. What do you say?"

The cat blinked up at him and let out a quiet meow. Somewhere in the back of Zander's mind, Allegra's voice resonated with a bittersweet lie.

This doesn't change anything.

The hell it didn't.

Grand Central Station was a tomb at five thirty in the morning.

Allegra's footsteps echoed on the smooth marble floor as she crossed the length of the quiet main concourse. The Tiffany-blue celestial ceiling loomed overhead, an infinite sky.

But it wasn't infinite. It wasn't even a sky. It was an illusion, much like her early-morning escape from Zander's bed. She'd thought if she left while he was still asleep it would lessen the pain of parting. For both of them.

Oh, how wrong she'd been. Her heart was in her throat, and there was an emptiness inside her like she'd never known. Worse than grief. Worse than having her world ripped out from under her. Because fate hadn't caused this terrible chasm, not this time. This time she'd plunged the knife into her own heart.

She'd done it again. She'd run away. Not because she wanted to, but because she had to. It was becoming something of a habit.

Her gaze snagged on the four-faced opal clock in the center of the terminal—5:35 a.m. Was Zander awake yet? Had he realized she'd gone?

He would be furious, and he had every right to feel that way. It had been the only way, though. If she'd had to look him in the eye and tell him goodbye just hours after he'd been inside her, she never would have gone. And then what?

Then you could have stayed.

No.

She bit down hard on the inside of her cheek and hauled her dance bag farther up on her shoulder. If she stayed, she'd live in constant fear of losing everything she held dear. The panic attacks would come back. She'd lose every last shred of control over her life.

No attachment, no fear. She'd go on tour with the dance company. She'd sleep in a different city every night, without strings and without the kind of emotional entanglements that threatened to pull her back into a place of unfathomable vulnerability. She'd be fine. She'd be safe.

She'd be alone.

Zander's voice rose, unbidden, to the forefront of her consciousness.

You can't even commit to a stray cat. That's no way to live, Allegra.

She swallowed, gulped a lungful of air and then swallowed again. Her stomach churned. Bile rose to the back of her throat. It tasted bitter and black, like the worst fear possible. Like panic.

Not now. Please not now.

She glanced around, as her heart raged inside her chest and a deep, sudden chill knifed through her body.

Her hands shook. Her feet began to tingle, and she had trouble taking a step.

Her surroundings blurred around the edges and tipped sideways, until the Tiffany-blue ceiling became the floor. She collided with a few commuters, before stumbling toward a wall and slumping against it as she slid to the ground.

She pressed her face to the wall's cool marble surface and closed her eyes.

Another panic attack.

Why?

This wasn't supposed to be happening. There was nothing to be afraid of anymore. She'd beaten fate to the punch. She'd willingly given up the opportunity to be gutted by loss.

But it found me, anyway.

She wasn't sure how long she sat there, paralyzed by fear. By regret. By the sinking realization that she'd just made the biggest mistake of her life. A half hour? An hour? Maybe longer.

She thought she might die, surrounded by strangers in a place where people came and went, running toward life while she'd been trying too hard to run away. Eventually her heartbeat slowed to normal, and she was able to take a breath and release it without choking. She dragged herself to her feet and staggered to the closest bathroom.

Inside the stall, she pulled her cell phone out of her dance bag to check the time. Had she missed her train?

But her phone was dead. She'd been so busy with the dance marathon she hadn't charged it in days. Perfect. Just perfect.

She tucked it back in her bag, splashed water on her

face and headed back to the concourse. She turned toward the legendary clock, its four opal faces glowing pale gold, awash in snowy morning light streaming through the grand arched windows.

Then she froze.

She blinked, convinced she was seeing things. Perhaps her panic attack had been more severe than she realized, because her imagination had taken over. Her wildest dream was somehow standing in front of her.

Zander was right there, next to the clock. Waiting. Waiting as patiently as if they'd agreed to meet there and embark on a long journey together. He held the little black kitten tucked into the crook of his elbow, and a white bakery bag dangled from his other hand—the kind they'd once used to collect Valentine's Day cards when they were children.

Was this real?

"Going somewhere?" he asked, arching an eyebrow.

"Um, yes." What was she saying? This was a miracle. He'd come for her. She'd done everything she could to push him away. She'd left him in the cruelest way possible, and here he was. She couldn't run anymore.

She didn't *want* to run.

She cleared her throat and gave him a wobbly smile. "I mean, no. It seems I've had a change of heart."

His lips curved in to a satisfied smile. "I hope that's true, because you disappeared this morning before I had a chance to wish you a happy birthday."

Her birthday.

She'd completely forgotten.

"You remembered." She shook her head. "With everything that's happened lately, it slipped my mind."

"Not mine. This day has been marked on my calendar

for more than a decade. We had a deal, remember? And that deal ends today." He offered her the bakery bag.

She took it with a shaky hand, afraid to look inside. Afraid that none of this was real and in a minute she'd wake up to find she'd been dreaming.

"Open it." There was a rough tenderness to his voice all of a sudden, as if he, too, feared it might be nothing but a perfect, wistful daydream.

It wasn't. It was real—as real as the platinum engagement ring that circled the candle atop the pink cupcake nestled inside the bag.

"Zander?" She stared down at the diamond nestled on a perfect swirl of frosting. She took a few deep breaths, until she finally trusted herself to reach inside the bag and retrieve the tiny cake without dropping it.

She did, and when she looked back up, Zander was down on one knee, gazing up at her as if she'd never run, as if he'd known all along she'd eventually find her way back to him.

"I've been waiting for this day since we were sixteen years old, Allegra. And I never stopped loving you. I can't promise you that you'll never lose anyone again. But I can promise you that as long as I live, I'll be your home." The kitten mewed, as if putting an exclamation point on the most beautiful proposal she could have imagined. Zander smiled and finished with the question she couldn't wait to answer. "Will you marry me?"

"Yes," she whispered.

Then, in the shadow of a clock that had welcomed soldiers returning from war and travelers who'd finally reached the end of long weary road, Allegra Clark threw her arms around Zander Wilde.

At long last, she'd come home.

* * *

Zander slid his arms into his tuxedo jacket and checked the time on his Cartier—11:00 p.m.

In an hour, Allegra's birthday would be over. Time was running out if they wanted to marry before the expiration of their childhood deal. And they most definitely did.

They'd toyed with the idea of heading straight from Grand Central Station to city hall. But they'd waited a lifetime to marry each other, and they wanted to do it right.

It just so happened the Bennington ballroom was available. Ryan and Emily had insisted on the ceremony's late hour in order to put together something special. *A proper wedding*, his mother had said. Allegra deserved to feel like a bride, and Zander couldn't argue.

But he was more than ready to make things official. He wanted Allegra in his life, and in his bed, permanently.

"Everything's all set." Ryan strode into Zander's office and looked him up and down. "It appears you're ready, as well."

Probably because he'd been waiting for this day since he was barely old enough to get his driver's license. "I am."

"Excellent. Celestia just arrived, and everyone else is seated. Let's do this." Ryan headed back out the door and down the Bennington's long hallway.

For a moment, Zander was stunned into inactivity. When he recovered, he caught up with Ryan in just a handful of large purposeful strides. "Hold up. What did you just say?"

"I said let's do this."

"Not that part." Zander raked a hand through his hair. "The part about Celestia Lane."

"Oh. What about it?" Ryan crossed his arms. His expression was perfectly neutral, as if this was the most mundane conversation in the world.

"What's she doing here?" Zander hissed.

"I called and invited her. I *had* to. We promised her a scoop on the next wedding to take place at the Bennington, and this is it."

Seriously?

It took every ounce of restraint Zander could muster not to wring his cousin's neck. Or better yet, fire him. Celestia Lane was the last person he wanted at his wedding. The very last.

He has a point, though.

As much as Zander hated to admit it, Ryan was right. If the reporter heard about this wedding after the fact, she'd accuse him of hiding something. She'd probably call an end to their truce and renew her negative reporting on the hotel and the absurd curse.

He'd given her his word. He'd even reiterated his promise as recently as last night.

He was stuck.

At the moment, he couldn't have cared less about the hotel. He was about to exchange vows with Allegra. But Celestia Lane was already there, and as promised, she had a photographer in tow.

Ryan looked up from fastening one of his cuff links and frowned. "You don't look well. Actually, that's an understatement. You look downright sick. Don't tell me you're getting cold feet. The last thing we need right now is *another* curse."

Zander glared at him.

Ryan shrugged one shoulder. Was that an actual *smirk* on his face? "Although *runaway groom* has a rather unique twist to it. It sounds classic, but unexpected. Don't you think?"

"I think I'm going to pummel you. That's what I think," Zander said.

Ryan clamped a hand on his shoulder and pulled him into a one-armed hug. His expression turned earnest. "You don't need to worry, cousin. She's not going to run."

Zander swallowed. "Am I that easy to read?"

"Not typically, but in this instance, yes."

"It's not the hotel I'm concerned about. You know that, right?" The Bennington would survive, no matter what happened tonight in the ballroom. It had been around since 1924. If the hotel could withstand the Great Depression, it could handle a few runaway brides.

That's what he'd been telling himself since the curse rumors had started, anyway.

If Allegra changed her mind about marrying him, the hotel would be fine.

His heart wouldn't.

"I know," Ryan said quietly.

"I'm in love with her." Zander shook his head. "I'm not sure I can remember a time when I wasn't."

"I know that, too." Ryan eyed a passing waiter carrying a tray of champagne. "Shall I get you a drink?"

"No, I'll be fine. The curse is messing with my head all of a sudden. That's all."

He and Allegra belonged together. For all practical purposes, he was betting his hotel on that fact. He would have bet his life on it, too, in a heartbeat.

What was about to take place beneath the ballroom's glittering indigo sky had been set in motion over a decade ago. He'd been a teenager back then, barely more than a kid. But when he'd turned his gaze on Allegra that day at the museum and suggested they marry when they were older, he hadn't been offering her a backup plan. It might have sounded like that's what he meant, but it wasn't. He knew neither of them would marry anyone else. The idea was inconceivable.

He might have stumbled over the words, but his intention had been clear. He wanted to marry Allegra. She was his dance partner, his confidante, his friend. He wanted them to be more. So much more.

Forever.

"I don't think the curse is messing with your head." Ryan buttoned his tux jacket and gave his bow tie a final tweak. "You know why?"

"Don't keep me in suspense," Zander said.

Ryan grinned. "Because you're forgetting something very important. There *is* no curse."

Zander laughed. "Touché."

"Now, let's go get you married." Ryan jerked his head in the direction of the ballroom.

Zander had seen the Bennington ballroom more times than he could count. He'd seen countless couples get married beneath its massive shimmering chandelier, from royalty to movie stars to heads of state. But he'd never seen the space look as breathtaking as it did right then.

Pale pink roses and orchids cascaded from the ceiling. The floor was covered with a blanket of flower petals. The lights were turned down low, and hundreds of white candles flanked the aisle leading up to the spot where he took his place and waited for the bridal march to begin.

But the surroundings paled in comparison to the beautiful sight of Allegra entering the room, bathed in candlelight, with a crown of flowers in her hair and stars in her eyes. Her dress was simple, elegant, with a bodice that looked almost like a dancer's leotard and a frothy skirt of layer upon layer of delicate tulle. She'd never looked more balletic, more lovely.

Deep in Zander's soul, a single word took root.

Mine.

In the end, he paid no attention whatsoever to Celestia Lane and her photographer. He barely even noticed his family members, although they were all there. His mother. Chloe. Tessa and Julian. Ryan, too, of course. He escorted Allegra down the aisle in place of her father.

But Zander only had eyes for his bride. She was exquisite. She was his. And for what felt like the first time since the day she'd lost everything, she was walking straight toward him instead of away.

She never looked back.

Not once.

She put one foot in front of the other and walked headlong into her future, *their* future, leaving the past behind.

Epilogue

The New York Times
Vows Exclusive Report

Bennington Hotel CEO Marries Childhood Sweetheart in Intimate Ceremony, Putting Curse Rumors to Rest

The Bennington Hotel's runaway bride curse is no longer.

Manhattan hotel king Zander Wilde wedded ballerina Allegra Clark late last night in the Bennington's famous starlight ballroom, surrounded by misty-eyed family members.

The bride and groom met when they were just nine years old, paired together as ballroom dance partners. After more than a decade apart, they recently reconnected on Mr. Wilde's thirtieth birthday in the very same ballroom where they tied the knot.

Yesterday wasn't just their wedding day, but also the bride's birthday. Wedding guests were treated to both a wedding cake and birthday cupcakes from Magnolia Bakery after the private ceremony.

The newlyweds plan to make their home in Manhattan, where the groom will continue at the helm of the Bennington and the bride will serve as codirector of the Wilde School of Dance.

When asked about the city's fascination with the hotel's curse, the groom declined to comment and instead referred us to the Bennington's Chief Financial Officer, Ryan Wilde. The dashing CFO assured Vows that romance is alive and well at the legendary hotel. To which we respond…

Might Ryan be the next Wilde to take a trip down the aisle?

* * * * *

Turn the page for a sneak peek at the latest entry in New York Times *bestselling author* *RaeAnne Thayne's* HAVEN POINT *series,* *THE COTTAGES ON SILVER BEACH, the story of a disgraced FBI agent, his best friend's sister and the loss that affected the trajectory of both their lives, available July 2018 wherever HQN books and ebooks are sold!*

CHAPTER ONE

SOMEONE WAS TRYING to bust into the cottages next door.

Only minutes earlier, Megan Hamilton had been minding her own business, sitting on her front porch, gazing out at the stars and enjoying the peculiar quiet sweetness of a late-May evening on Lake Haven. She had earned this moment of peace after working all day at the inn's front desk then spending the last four hours at her computer, editing photographs from Joe and Lucy White's fiftieth anniversary party the weekend before.

Her neck was sore, her shoulders tight, and she simply wanted to savor the purity of the evening with her dog at her feet. Her moment of Zen had lasted only sixty seconds before her little ancient pug, Cyrus, sat up, gazed out into the darkness and gave one small harrumphing noise before settling back down again to watch as a vehicle pulled up to the cottage next door.

Cyrus had become used to the comings and goings of their guests in the two years since he and Megan moved into the cottage after the inn's renovations were finished. She would venture to say her pudgy little dog seemed to actually enjoy the parade of strangers who invariably stopped to greet him.

The man next door wasn't aware of her presence,

though, or that of her little pug. He was too busy trying to work the finicky lock—not an easy feat as the task typically took two hands and one of his appeared to be attached to an arm tucked into a sling.

She should probably go help him. He was obviously struggling one-handed, unable to turn the key and twist the knob at the same time.

Beyond common courtesy, there was another compelling reason she should probably get off her porch swing and assist him. He was a guest of the inn, which meant he was yet one more responsibility on her shoulders. She knew the foibles of that door handle well, since she owned the door, the porch, the house and the land that it sat on, here at Silver Beach on Lake Haven, part of the extensive grounds of the Inn at Haven Point.

She didn't want to help him. She wanted to stay right here hidden in shadows, trying to pretend he wasn't there. Maybe this was all a bad dream and she wouldn't be stuck with him for the next three weeks.

Megan closed her eyes, wishing she could open them again and find the whole thing was a figment of her imagination.

Unfortunately, it was all entirely too real. Elliot Bailey. Living next door.

She didn't want him here. Stupid online bookings. If he had called in person about renting the cottage next to hers—one of five small, charming two-bedroom vacation rentals along the lakeshore—she might have been able to concoct some excuse.

With her imagination, surely she could have come up with something good. All the cottages were being painted. A plumbing issue meant none of them had water. The entire place had to be fumigated for tarantulas.

If she had spoken with him in person, she might have been able to concoct *some* excuse that would keep Elliot Bailey away. But he had used the inn's online reservation system and paid in full before she even realized who was moving in next door. Now she was stuck with him for three entire weeks.

She would have to make the best of it.

As he tried the door again, guilt poked at her. Even if she didn't want him here, she couldn't sit here when one of her guests needed help. It was rude, selfish and irresponsible. "Stay," she murmured to Cyrus, then stood up and made her way down the porch steps of Primrose Cottage and back up those of Cedarwood.

"May I help?"

At her words, Elliot whirled around, the fingers of his right hand flexing inside his sling as if reaching for a weapon. She had to hope he didn't have one. Maybe she should have thought of that before sneaking up on him.

Elliot was a decorated FBI agent and always exuded an air of cold danger, as if ready to strike at any moment. It was as much a part of him as his blue eyes.

His brother had shared the same eyes, but the similarities between them ended there. Wyatt's blue eyes had been warm, alive, brimming with personality. Elliot's were serious and solemn and always seemed to look at her as if she were some kind of alien life-form that had landed in his world.

Her heart gave a familiar pinch at the thought of

Wyatt and the fledgling dreams that had been taken away from her on a snowy road.

"Megan," he said, his voice as stiff and formal as if he were greeting J. Edgar Hoover himself. "I didn't see you."

"It's a dark evening and I'm easy to miss. I didn't mean to startle you."

In the yellow glow of the porch light, his features appeared lean and alert, like a hungry mountain lion. She could feel her muscles tense in response, a helpless doe caught unawares in an alpine meadow.

She adored the rest of the Bailey family. All of them, even linebacker-big Marshall. Why was Elliot the only one who made her so blasted nervous?

"May I help you?" she asked again. "This lock can be sticky. Usually it takes two hands, one to twist the key and the other to pull the door toward you."

"That could be an issue for the next three weeks." His voice seemed flat and she had the vague, somewhat disconcerting impression that he was tired. Elliot always seemed so invincible but now lines bracketed his mouth and his hair was uncharacteristically rumpled. It seemed so odd to see him as anything other than perfectly controlled.

Of course he was tired. The man had just driven in from Denver. Anybody would be exhausted after an eight-hour drive—especially when he was healing from an obvious injury and probably in pain.

What happened to his arm? She wanted to ask, but couldn't quite find the courage. It wasn't her business, anyway. Elliot was a guest of her inn and deserved all the hospitality she offered to any guest—including whatever privacy he needed and help accessing the cottage he had paid in advance to rent.

"There is a trick," she told him. "If you pull the door slightly toward you first, then turn the key, you should be able to manage with one hand. If you have trouble again, you can find me or one of the staff to help you. I live next door."

The sound he made might have been a laugh or a scoff. She couldn't tell.

"Of course you do."

She frowned. What did that mean? With all the renovations to the inn after a devastating fire, she couldn't afford to pay for an overnight manager. It had seemed easier to move into one of the cottages so she could be close enough to step in if the front desk clerks had a problem in the middle of the night.

That's the only reason she was here. Elliot didn't need to respond to that information as if she was some loser who hadn't been able to fly far from the nest.

"We need someone on-site full-time to handle emergencies," she said stiffly. "Such as guests who can't open their doors by themselves."

"I am certainly not about to bother you or your staff every time I need to go in and out of my own rental unit. I'll figure something out."

His voice sounded tight, annoyed, and she tried to attribute it to travel weariness instead of that subtle disapproval she always seemed to feel emanating from him.

"I can help you this time at least." She inserted his key, exerted only a slight amount of pull on the door and heard the lock disengage. She pushed the door open and flipped on a light inside the cheery little two-bedroom cottage, with its small combined living-dining room and kitchen table set in front of the big windows overlooking the lake.

"Thank you for your help," he said, sounding a little less censorious.

"Anytime." She smiled her well-practiced, smooth, innkeeper smile. After a decade of running the twenty-room Inn at Haven Point on her own, she had become quite adept at exuding hospitality she was far from feeling.

"May I help you with your bags?"

He gave her a long, steady look that conveyed clearly what he thought of that offer. "I'm good. Thanks."

She shrugged. Stubborn man. Let him struggle. "Good night, then. If you need anything, you know where to find me."

"Yes. I do. Next door, apparently."

"That's right. Good night," she said again, then returned to her front porch, where she and Cyrus settled in to watch him pull a few things out of his vehicle and carry them inside.

She could have saved him a few trips up and down those steps, but clearly he wanted to cling to his own stubbornness instead. As usual, it was obvious he wanted nothing to do with her. Elliot tended to treat her as if she were a riddle he had no desire to solve.

Over the years, she had developed pretty good strategies for avoiding him at social gatherings, though it was a struggle. She had once been almost engaged to his younger brother. That alone would tend to link her to the Bailey family, but it wasn't the only tie between them. She counted his sisters, Wynona Bailey Emmett and Katrina Bailey Callahan, among her closest friends.

In fact, because of her connection to his sisters, she knew he was in town at least partly to attend a big after-the-fact reception to celebrate Katrina's wedding to Bowie Callahan, which had been a small destination event in Colombia several months earlier.

Megan had known Elliot for years. Though only five or six years older, somehow he had always seemed ancient to her, even when she was a girl—as if he belonged to some earlier generation. He was so serious all the time, like some sort of stuffy uncle who couldn't be bothered with youthful shenanigans.

Hey, you kids. Get off my lawn.

He'd probably never actually said those words, but she could clearly imagine them coming out of that incongruously sexy mouth.

He did love his family. She couldn't argue that. He watched out for his sisters and was close to his brother Marshall, the sheriff of Lake Haven County. He cherished his mother and made the long trip from Denver to Haven Point for every important Bailey event, several times a year.

Which also begged the question, why had he chosen to rent a cottage on the inn property instead of staying with one of his family members?

His mother and stepfather lived not far away and so did Marshall, Wynona and Katrina with their respective spouses. While Marshall's house was filled to the brim with kids, Cade and Wyn had plenty of room and Bowie and Katrina had a vast house on Serenity Harbor that would fit the entire Haven Point High School football team, with room left over for the coaching staff and a few cheerleaders.

Instead, Elliot had chosen to book this small, solitary rental unit at the inn for three entire weeks.

Did his reasons have anything to do with that sling? How had he been hurt? Did it have anything to do with his work for the FBI?

None of her business, Megan reminded herself. He was a guest at her inn, which meant she had an obligation to respect his privacy.

He came back to the vehicle for one more bag, something that looked the size of a laptop, which gave her something else to consider. He had booked the cottage for three weeks. Maybe he had taken a leave of absence or something to work on another book.

She pulled Cyrus into her lap and rubbed behind his ears as she considered the cottage next door and the enigmatic man currently inhabiting it. Whoever would have guessed that the stiff, humorless, focused FBI agent could pen gripping true crime books in his spare time? She would never admit it to Elliot, but she found it utterly fascinating how his writing managed to convey pathos and drama and even some lighter moments.

True crime was definitely not her groove at all but she had read his last bestseller in five hours, without so much as stopping to take a bathroom break—and had slept with her closet light on for weeks.

That still didn't mean she wanted him living next door. At this point, she couldn't do anything to change that. The only thing she could do was treat him with the same courtesy and respect she would any other guest at the inn.

No matter how difficult that might prove.

What the hell was he doing here?

Elliot dragged his duffel to the larger of the cottage's two bedrooms, where a folding wood-framed luggage stand had been set out, ready for guests.

The cottage was tastefully decorated in what he termed Western chic—bold mission furniture, wood plank ceiling, colorful rugs on the floor. A river rock fireplace dominated the living room, probably perfect for those chilly evenings along the lakeshore.

Cedarwood Cottage seemed comfortable and welcoming, a good place for him to huddle over his laptop and pound out the last few chapters of the book that was overdue to his editor.

Even so, he could already tell this was a mistake.

Why the hell hadn't he just told his mother and Katrina he couldn't make it to the reception? He'd flown to Cartagena for the wedding three months earlier after all. Surely that showed enough personal commitment to his baby sister's nuptials.

They would have protested but would have understood—and in the end it wouldn't have much mattered whether he made it home for the event or not. The reception wasn't about him, it was about Bowie and Katrina and the life they were building with Bowie's younger brother Milo and Kat's adopted daughter, Gabriella.

For his part, Elliot was quite sure he would have been better off if he had stayed holed up in his condo in Denver to finish the book, no matter how awkward things had become for him there. If he closed the blinds, ignored the doorbell and just hunkered down, he could have typed one-handed or even dictated the changes he needed to make. The whole thing would have been done in a week.

The manuscript wasn't the problem.

Elliot frowned, his head pounding in rhythm to each throbbing ache of his shoulder.

He was the problem—and he couldn't escape the mess he had created, no matter how far away from Denver he drove.

He struggled to unzip the duffel one-handed, then finally gave up and stuck his right arm out of the sling to help. His shoulder ached even more in response, not happy with being subjected to eight hours of driving only days postsurgery.

How was he going to explain the shoulder injury to his mother? He couldn't tell her he was recovering from a gunshot wound. Charlene had lost a son and husband in the line of duty and had seen both a daughter and her other son injured on the job.

And he certainly couldn't tell Marshall or Cade about all the trouble he was in. He was the model FBI agent, with the unblemished record.

Until now.

Unpacking took him all of five minutes, moving the packing cubes into drawers, setting his toiletries in the bathroom, hanging the few dress shirts he had brought along. When he was done, he wandered back into the combined living room/kitchen.

The front wall was made almost entirely of windows, perfect for looking out and enjoying the spectacular view of Lake Haven during one of its most beautiful seasons, late spring, before the tourist horde descended.

On impulse, Elliot walked out onto the wide front porch. The night was chilly but the mingled scents of pine and cedar and lake intoxicated him. He drew fresh mountain air deep into his lungs.

This.

If he needed to look for a reason why he had been compelled to come home during his suspension and the investigation into his actions, he only had to think about what this view would look like in the morning, with the sun creeping over the mountains.

Lake Haven called to him like nowhere else on Earth—not just the stunning blue waters or the mountains that jutted out of them in jagged peaks but the calm, rhythmic lapping of the water against the shore, the ever-changing sky, the cry of wood ducks pedaling in for a landing.

He had spent his entire professional life digging into the worst aspects of the human condition, investigating cruelty and injustice and people with no moral conscience whatsoever. No matter what sort of muck he waded through, he had figured out early in his career at the FBI that he could keep that ugliness from touching the core of him with thoughts of Haven Point and the people he loved who called this place home.

He didn't visit as often as he would like. Between his job at the Denver field office and the six true crime books he had written, he didn't have much free time.

That all might be about to change. He might have more free time than he knew what to do with.

His shoulder throbbed again and he adjusted the sling, gazing out at the stars that had begun to sparkle above the lake.

After hitting rock bottom professionally, with his entire future at the FBI in doubt, where else would he come but home?

He sighed and turned to go back inside. As he did, he spotted the lights still gleaming at the cottage next door, with its blue trim and the porch swing overlooking the water.

She wasn't there now.

Megan Hamilton. Auburn hair, green eyes, a smile that always seemed soft and genuine to everyone else but him.

He drew in a breath, aware of a sharp little twinge of hunger deep in his gut.

When he booked the cottage, he hadn't really thought things through. He should have remembered that Megan and the Inn at Haven Point were a package deal. She owned the inn along with these picturesque little guest cottages on Silver Beach.

He had no idea she actually *lived* in one herself, though. If he had ever heard that little fact, he had forgotten it. Should he have remembered, he would have looked a little harder for a short-term rental property, rather than picking the most convenient lakeshore unit he had found.

Usually, Elliot did his best to avoid her. He wasn't sure why but Megan always left him…unsettled. It had been that way for ages, since long before he learned she and his younger brother had started dating.

He could still remember his shock when he came

home for some event or other and saw her and Wyatt together. As in, together, together. Holding hands, sneaking the occasional kiss, giving each other secret smiles. Elliot had felt as if Wyatt had peppered him with buckshot.

He had tried to be happy for his younger brother, one of the most generous, helpful, loving people he'd ever known. Wyatt had been a genuinely good person and deserved to be happy with someone special.

Elliot had felt small and selfish for wishing that someone hadn't been Megan Hamilton.

Watching their glowing happiness together had been tough. He had stayed away for the four or five months they had been dating, though he tried to convince himself it hadn't been on purpose. Work had been demanding and he had been busy carving out his place in the Bureau. He had also started the research that would become his first book, looking into a long-forgotten Montana case from a century earlier where a man had wooed, then married, then killed three spinster schoolteachers from back East for their life insurance money before finally being apprehended by a savvy local sheriff and the sister of one of the dead women.

The few times Elliot returned home during the time Megan had been dating his brother, he had been forced to endure family gatherings knowing she would be there, upsetting his equilibrium and stealing any peace he usually found here.

He couldn't let her do it to him this time.

Her porch light switched off a moment later and Elliot finally breathed a sigh of relief.

He would only be here three weeks. Twenty-one

days. Despite the proximity of his cabin to hers, he likely wouldn't even see her much, other than at Katrina's reception.

She would be busy with the inn, with her photography, with her wide circle of friends, while he should be focused on finishing his manuscript and allowing his shoulder to heal—not to mention figuring out whether he would still have a career at the end of that time.

Don't miss THE COTTAGES ON SILVER BEACH
by RaeAnne Thayne,
available July 2018
wherever HQN books and ebooks are sold!

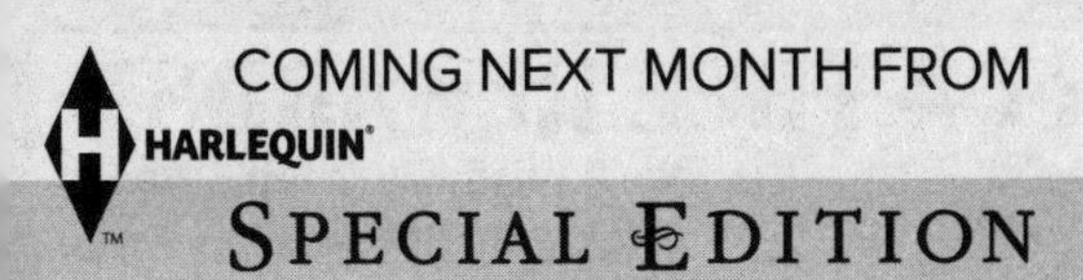

Available July 17, 2018

#2635 THE MAVERICK'S BABY-IN-WAITING
Montana Mavericks: The Lonelyhearts Ranch • by Melissa Senate
After dumping her cheating fiancé, mom-to-be Mikayla Brown is trying to start fresh—without a man!—but Jensen Jones is determined to pursue her. He's not ready to be a daddy...or is he?

#2636 ADDING UP TO FAMILY
Matchmaking Mamas • by Marie Ferrarella
When widowed rocket scientist Steve Holder needs a housekeeper who can help with his precocious ten-year-old, The Matchmaking Mamas know just who to call! But Becky Reynolds soon finds herself in over her head—and on the path to gaining a family!

#2637 SHOW ME A HERO
American Heroes • by Allison Leigh
When small-town cop Ali Templeton shows up at Grant Cooper's door with a baby she says is his niece, the air force vet turned thriller writer is surprised by more than the baby—there's an undeniable attraction to deal with, too. Can he be a hero for more than just the baby's sake? Or will Ali be left out in the cold once again?

#2638 THE BACHELOR'S BABY SURPRISE
Wilde Hearts • by Teri Wilson
After a bad breakup and a one-night stand, Evangeline Holly just wants to forget the whole thing. But it turns out Ryan Wilde is NYC's hottest bachelor, her new boss—and the father of her child!

#2639 HER LOST AND FOUND BABY
The Daycare Chronicles • by Tara Taylor Quinn
Tabitha Jones has teamed up with her food-truck-running neighbor, Johnny Brubaker, to travel to different cities to find her missing son. But as they get closer to bringing Jackson back, they have to decide if they really want their time together to come to an end...

#2640 HIGH COUNTRY COWGIRL
The Brands of Montana • by Joanna Sims
Bonita Delafuente has deferred her dreams to care for her mother. Is falling for Gabe Brand going to force her to choose between love and medical school? Or will her medical history make the choice for her?

When small-town cop Ali Templeton finds the uncle of an abandoned infant, she wasn't expecting a famous author—or an undeniable attraction!

Read on for a sneak preview of the next book in the ***AMERICAN HEROES*** *miniseries,*
SHOW ME A HERO,
by New York Times *bestselling author* Allison Leigh.

"Are you going to ask when you can meet your niece?"

Grant grimaced. "You don't know that she's my niece. You only think she is."

"It's a pretty good hunch," Ali continued. "If you're willing to provide a DNA sample, we could know for sure."

His DNA wouldn't prove squat, though he had no intention of telling her that. Particularly now that they'd become the focus of everyone inside the bar. The town had a whopping population of 5,000. Maybe. It was small, but that didn't mean there wasn't a chance he'd be recognized. And the last thing he wanted was a rabid fan showing up on his doorstep.

He'd had too much of that already. It was one of the reasons he'd taken refuge at the ranch that his biological grandparents had once owned. He'd picked it up for a song when it was auctioned off years ago, but he hadn't seriously entertained doing much of anything with it—especially living there himself.

HSEEXP0718

At the time, he'd just taken perverse pleasure in being able to buy up the place where he'd never been welcomed while they'd been alive.

Now it was in such bad disrepair that to stay there even temporarily, he'd been forced to make it habitable.

He wondered if Karen had stayed there, unbeknownst to him. If she was responsible for any of the graffiti or the holes in the walls.

He pushed away the thought and focused on the officer. "Ali. What's it short for?"

She hesitated, obviously caught off guard. "Alicia, but nobody ever calls me that." He'd been edging closer to the door, but she'd edged right along with him. "So, about that—"

Her first name hadn't been on the business card she'd left for him. "Ali fits you better than Alicia."

She gave him a look from beneath her just-from-bed sexy bangs. "Stop changing the subject, Mr. Cooper."

"Start talking about something else, then. Better yet—" he gestured toward the bar and Marty "—start doing the job you've gotta be getting paid for since I can't imagine you slinging drinks just for the hell of it."

Her eyes narrowed and her lips thinned. "Mr. Cooper—"

"G'night, Officer Ali." He pushed open the door and headed out into the night.

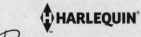